NU-PIKE PRESS

TRUE STORIES

A LOOSE COLLECTION OF
FLASH FICTION

NU-PIKE PRESS

TRUE STORIES
Copyright 2023 by Jack Grisham

All rights reserved.
Printed in the United States of America.

For information address:
Nu-Pike Press, P.O. Box 735
Huntington Beach, California 92648
nupikepress@gmail.com
+1 (714)-794-5625

Editor
Melissa Elhardt

Additional Editing
Lucas Kutner

Cover Art
Julia Kwong

An Introduction

The short stories you're about to read are quick, angry, blasphemous—and sure to trigger your sensitive issues. They're also dirty. If it takes you more than five minutes to get through one, you're jerking off.

Some call this style *flash fiction*—short thousand-word hits. I call it, *literary adultery*—amusement for creeps.

Let's say you've got one of the classics on your nightstand—Great Expectations maybe, or the wondrous Ulysses. You've been seeing each other for a few weeks. You're devoted. You wouldn't mind your friends knowing who you were with. At night, you fall asleep with it cradled in your arms. The godlike passages sing you to sleep, lifting your dreams to heaven.

It's beautiful, lofty, and after a few hundred pages... a fucking bore.

You need excitement. You need that nasty soft-cover bitch who'll do all the things your classic won't. You need a bareback romp through six by nine pages of steamy, late-night trash.

Picture this: while your classic waits patiently for your return, you casually cruise by this collection—this cheap, short jolt in the junk. It winks at you from across the room. It doesn't want commitment. It's got other lovers, other hands to lie in. It only wants a few filthy moments of your time. You look over your shoulder—no one watching—you wouldn't want your reputation as a deep thinker tarnished, and you reach for it.

The cover is stained and torn—it's greasy, and there's a heat emanating from within. You crack its spine. The words jump from the pages like a midnight bang in the backseat of your father's car.

It's wham, bam, thank you mam, and it's over. A quick kiss goodbye. Clean yourself up. Return to your classic.

Your tired old lover is none the wiser.

In Loving Memory of...

Fix Me

It didn't matter that she wasn't a therapist, or that the information she quoted came from a podcast—the name of which she couldn't remember.

It didn't matter that she wore high-waisted pants—her vagina a foot below the top button. That her legs were too short, her torso too long.

None of it mattered. Because at that moment, I was uncomfortable. And she was there.

"You're afraid of rejection," she said. "You gravitate to women who need you—not ones who are whole and want you. I think you should abstain for a while. Refrain from sexual contact. Give yourself a chance to find out who you really are."

"Oh, so that's what this is? You want to know who I've been fucking? Fine.

"I've been fucking single mothers, newcomers, and women who can't pay their rent. I sleep with the unwanted—the bitches on benders. Any semi-attractive, needy woman looking for sick validation through a man like me.

"That's who I'm fucking.

"They're easy.

"But before you start getting all Freud on me—I'm not deceiving anyone. I give myself to each of them, honestly.

"And maybe—if I'm deft enough with my touch—the orgasm that I bestow might ease their pain, at least long enough to help them survive this dark and seemingly endless journey that they've found themselves on.

"And if they ever do stumble onto a sliver of hope or purpose, I'm sure they'll have the strength to live with the fact that all I gave them was a cock, a soft touch, a little intelligent conversation, and an inability to cum… yet still stay hard.

"I know who I am.

"I'm a fucking crusader."

"You sound like a narcissist."

"And you, dear, sound like my second ex-wife. I'm not a narcissist—neither am I a sociopath nor a psychopath. I'm what happens when you take a young boy who wanted nothing more than love and acceptance from his parents, and you give him lies, forced enemas, beatings, withhold affection, and tell him that you would be better off if he was dead. I'm not mentally ill. I am the consummate human—desperate to feel like he belongs.

You know, one time I was giving myself to this woman—single mother of three, drug addicted, on the state ticket—and right between pumps, I thought: why bother? Why should we comfort each other with our touch? Where in this shithole of humanity is there room for a suckled-on pig who offers nothing but more future addicts—and me, an artist who supposedly brightens lives, a force for good in my community. Pfttttt…Big fucking deal. In the grand scheme, it makes no difference if you add or subtract—the sum of human existence is always zero.

"Why should either of us seek one moment of pleasure? I'm wasting my time, and she's delaying the inevitable—for what? Her self-preservation. I should have O.D'd her and offed myself."

"I think therapy could work wonders—"

"Really? You got some balls on you, bitch—telling me I could benefit from therapy when you're wearing those jeans, and your advice is trickling out over a pair of too thin lips and a row of dead chicklet teeth."

"Why don't you stop being an asshole. If this is how you treat women that want you, no wonder you're alone."

"What? Hang on. What did you just say?"

"I said, I want you."

"You want me?"

"Yes. I want you to get better—for us. I'm not here because I need you. I'm here because I *want* you. I find you fascinating, and I'm okay—as is."

"As is? Are you fucking serious? If you were okay, why the fuck would you want me? If anyone were okay, why would they want anyone beside themselves?

"I don't want to be wanted. I don't want to wait for your calls or cruise your fucking social feed wondering what enlightened motherfucker's been pumping you full of semen-coated wisdom that you feel the need to drop in my lap.

"I don't want *you*."

We sat silent—and unlike me, she was content to hover in that wordless space between us.

"The other day I was feeling tired—burned out—and to be honest, maybe a touch suicidal. So I figured I'd get it out online—lance the pain in a public forum, as it were.

"On my social media page, there was a little box that asked me, *What's on your mind?* Well, what was on my mind was that I'd like to wipe the slate clean and start over—go back to the beginning of my life with eyes of love and wonder instead of anger and doubt. I'd like to have never been a child who looked on the world with hope, only to have the reality of chaos and cruelty crush me.

"Those were the things on my mind—but there's no way those things ever come true. So my next thought was: the only way out is a fucking bullet in my brain. There is no purpose, no reason to exist on this planet except suffering.

"This website asked me, what's on my mind, when it's been proven—through analytics—that it already knows the answer. I'm just waiting for the day when I talk suicide and ads for euthanasia centers and lightweight pistols pop up in my newsfeed—just like pills for depression and erectile dysfunction do now.

"I'm fucking hurting. Am I selfish because I need to be touched? What am I supposed to do—stay alone until some therapist with a handful of antidepressants tells me I'm well enough to offer someone more than my body?

"Fuck that noise.

"When I get to my office, I'll have messages from women who've recently tried to kill themselves—and I'll return their calls. Because even if it hurts later—and according to you, I'm not gonna get better until I abstain from their touch—it's still a pair of arms around me. A body—albeit sick—lying next to me.

"It's still someone who needs me.

"And you sit there, and you say you *want* me."

I began to cry.

I needed the comfort of flesh on my flesh.

I reached for her…

"No," she said. "I can't fix you."

The Hustler

He wanted the money. At least that's what he told himself, but maybe there was some strange fascination too—boys of thirteen are often easily fascinated. Besides, his friend, George had done it. Eric too. And there'd been talk that the black kid in Jay's English class had also gone. It was a quick hundred bucks.

"What am I supposed to wear?"

"I don't know"—the voice on the other end laughed—"It's not a date."

"What'd you wear?"

"Are you shitting me? Jesus, Terry, I just wore what I had on."

"Did you shower?"

"Look, do whatever you want. I don't think he gives a fuck."

Terry threw on a pair of dirty jeans and a sweatshirt. He didn't bother showering—the old creep probably liked it dirty.

"Hey Mom, can you give me a ride to the mall? I'm meeting the guys at the movies."

"Did you clean your room?"

"Yeah, fed Roger and took out the trash too."

"You know, you really should walk him more—he is your dog."

The drive was silent. The older he got, the less he wanted to talk to the woman who cooked his meals. His father was practically non-existent. Oh, he was around, but Terry couldn't remember the last time they'd hung out. It was work, dinner, bed, and the occasional threat of discipline when "T-dog" wasn't performing up to snuff.

He dodged a quick kiss on the cheek—jumped out of the car and ran across the street to the mall. He walked past the arcade and did quick math on what he could buy with his pay.

If a man traveling to the mall at 25 mph gives you a head-job for five minutes, and games cost $40, how many games can you get for $100?

He was supposed to wait by the bike store—just stand there at 1p.m. and he'd come. It wasn't long before he showed.

"Are you Terry?"

At first it looked like trouble—the man who approached him wasn't a creep, more of a schoolteacher type. Reminded him of Mr. Weathers, the principal.

"Yes, sir." His parents had taught him to be polite to strangers—it wasn't wasted here.

"Great." The man looked him over. "They said you might be up for a job. You wanna take a walk?"

He followed him around to the alley behind the theatre. They walked down the steps toward the exit doors. It smelled like piss and puke—somebody'd been drinking.

Terry stood casual, hands in his pockets.

"Let me see what you got, son."

This was what he'd been told—that was the cue. He unbuttoned his jeans and waited.

The man got on his knees, grabbed Terry by the waist, and pulled him into his mouth. He groaned and moaned as he worked. Terry leaned back, palms against the cold concrete wall. The soundtrack of the movie wiggled under the cracks in the door—audience laughter crowding the dank alcove. The man pulled him closer. Terry felt like he had to piss. He couldn't hold it much longer. His body spasmed. He came. It was quick—and better than he expected.

The man slowly pulled away, savoring the moment. He stood, wiped his mouth with the back of his hand, and pulled a folded bill from his pocket.

"Here," he said, handing Terry the cash. "Put that in your kick."

Terry buttoned up and mumbled a thank you. He felt like he should say something more, but the man had already turned away. Without another word, he climbed the stairs to the alley.

It was easy money.

A Case of Mistaken Gender Identity

He walked into the local Lane Bryant and grabbed a pair of quadruple-X nylons—control top, for bigger girls.

And he was big—a solid two-hundred and eighty pounds of mostly fat piled high on a medium bone structure frame.

"Are you going out tonight?"

The nosey clerk at the counter made small talk as she rang him up.

"Girl, you know I am."

He was a liar.

It was also Halloween—a perfect cover for the cross-dressing gentleman.

"I'm going as one of those Hollywood actresses—"

He twirled around and fanned his ass.

"Guess which one?"

She laughed.

"You're Kim—no, you're the young one with the…uh…"

He grabbed his bag and headed for the door.

He was going to wait until he got home to dress, but the mile to his apartment seemed like forever. He ducked into an alley.

He removed from his bag a pair of size 12 flats—he'd tried heels once, but it was a disaster.

His ankle still hurt from the twist.

He unpacked a black Spandex dress and a red wig.

As for padding, he needed none.

He had womanly hips, and his push-up bra lifted his large man-tits to just about right.

That is, if you were looking to be a man not even half-close to passing.

He was ugly—yet desperate to be seen as the woman he felt himself to be.

He waddled out of the alley and took to the street.

Laughs and catcalls fell rudely upon him.

Two street corner boys played rough with his emotions.

"Hey, Baby! You got that dick all taped back?"

"Does your girl know you run off with her wig?"

He ignored their tired remarks.

He may not have been the prettiest girl on the street, but he knew he had more class than the hoes those creeps ran with.

He played his hands over his hips, smoothed his dress, and moved on.

A young boy, walking a bicycle, approached him.

"Excuse me, sir? Do you have the time?"

He employed the highest register of his voice—a raspy baritone.

"You're a very rude young man. Do I look as if I have a watch?"

He held out his hairy arms—his thick wrist unadorned.

"I'm sorry, dude. Just asking."

The boy laughed, hopped on his bike, and peddled away.

"I'm a woman goddamnit!"

His futile yell fell against the teen's back.

"What's with the youth these days? Rude and blind as bats."

He walked the main drag, and then turned up Chestnut to cut through the park. The depression that often followed crept up behind as he stopped to admire his reflection in a shop window.

Disappointment returned his gaze.

The wide jaw.

The dark 5 o'clock shadow—no matter how close the shave.

The large bulging Adam's apple bobbing as he sobbed.

"How could God make me so?" he whimpered.

"I want to be beautiful. I want the world to see the woman within."

"No one sees it. Not even you, fat boy." His reflection spoke in his father's voice. *"You're a sad, worthless faggot—good for nothing but a laugh."*

His manly tears stumbled down his pock-marked cheeks and clung to his stubble.

He was defeated.

"Fuck this," he said, as he reached up to discard his wig. "I'll never be a woman."

Bang! Bang!

Shots rang from behind—a disturbance in the liquor store.

Screams.

Windows shattering.

Bang! Bang!

He froze—terrified.

His red curls fixed in the afternoon sun.

A hopped-up John Washington Junior had just pegged the clerk, the stockboy, and two elderly matrons who were arguing over the price of tuna.

He snatched $272 dollars and fifty-five cents from Bonus Bob's Liquor Mart and ran for the connection, lickety split.

Outside, our boy held his place.

Trembling in his dress, he stood as John Jr. approached from behind.

By sad coincidence—at least to those who are wont to commit crimes—a police cruiser randomly appeared on the scene.

The unit broke hard into the corner.

Two officers jumped from within—guns at the ready.

"Get the fuck out of there!" the lead cop yelled.

Too late.

John Washington Junior had grabbed his girl and shoved the gun against her breast.

"Stay the fuck back," John screamed. "One move and the bitch gets it!"

The officers held.

John Washington Junior tightened his grip. His hot breath on her neck. His body pressed against hers.

Ecstatic, she leaned her head against his. Pushed back into his hips. Cherished his touch.

Finally—recognized as the woman she was meant to be.

The Writers

On one end there is Kerouac, and on the other, ten thousand foul-smelling hippies clogging coffee bars with unkempt hair and notebooks that reek of patchouli and bunk Mexican brown.

As for Bukowski, there was also just one—the Big Bukowski.

His imitators are nothing more than foul-mouthed, obnoxious "Hanks" wallowing in cheap booze and dusty beer-fart shenanigans.

I've heard them—talking their shit, bragging of their prowess with prose.

Bitch please, the only thing these wannabe writers are prolific at is urinating: fifteen-minute-long streams of 20-proof slop cascading from beer-shrunken cocks, voraciously gobbled up by water-saving-urinals.

Now, I'm not saying you fuckers shouldn't follow your dreams—your lifelong desire to be a writer—I support your futility.

I'm just saying you need to stop trying to recreate someone else's dream. Because unlike stars in the sky—each of which shine so heavenly—most of us are just human.

Dull lumps of God molded clay, destined for obscurity.

"Hey, what'cha doing, man?"

I smelled the foul stench before I looked up and into the glazed eyes of a traveler.

"You're a writer now, huh?"

"Nah, I'm a hack."

"What?"

"I mean, writing isn't my dream. I lived mine—I was a punk rock superstar, and now I document the memories of what I used to be.

"Sadly, most of them are lost in a maze of scar tissue and a cavalcade of lies I've concocted to hide the pain and inflate my ego."

"Wow, that's deep."

"Yes… it is. I am one deep motherfucker.

"As a matter of fact, I was just sitting here probing the depths of your existence."

"Mine?"

"Yep, right here"—I moved my hand away from the paper so he could get a glimpse—"it says that you unwashed travelers clog the coffee bars and bug the fuck out of me.

"So why don't you grab your dirty little chai, strap on your fucking tie-dyed backpack, and go have yourself a nice day."

I dismissed him to the street.

"I'm writing a book."

The voice that piped in was sitting two wooden chairs over—tight cotton T-shirt struggling to contain a set of aggressive titties—bumblebee lips, spray-tanned leatherette skin stretched skeleton-thin over altered cheekbones.

She'd been listening as I toyed with the Hippie.

"My girlfriends said I should write a 'Fifty Shades thing'—I've done some stuff."

I could smell the sour wine stink as she talked—her breath doing its best to secondhand-intoxicate me.

"Oh, so you've sucked a lot of cock, huh? Is that why you got your lips done?"

Her age-spotted fingers fluttered, indignant to her mouth.

"Did you ever get tied up—have a dildo the size of an elephant's trunk slammed up your rectum?"

"No, but I uh… "

"You know, my last girlfriend was also a hooker—she came down with a nasty case of vaginitis and it shut down business for the holidays.

"Hey, I got something you can write about—how much would you charge me to go suck off that traveler who just left? I'll buy you a latte and a lemon bar—that's gotta be good for a chapter or two."

"Fuck you, asshole."

Oh well, we can't all be writers, but we can inspire those that are— we can give them fodder as they cannon strike their way through life trying to enlighten those that strive to become other than themselves.

You have a nice day now.

It is your choice.

Bitch

He'd compiled a list of anyone who'd ever wronged him, and these names we're noted—line by line, in over 300 college-ruled notebooks he'd stored in his one-bedroom, adult assisted-living condo.

They were a bitch's accumulation of 53 years.

His latest wrongdoer was Tom, the new man at work—the middle-aged pretty-boy who thrilled the girls and glad-handed the bosses.

Tom had slighted Edgar in the cafeteria—a matter of a French fry picked from his plate.

"Oh, if the people at work could only see Tom as he really was—large, greedy hands snatching and grabbing without a thought for others."

"Edgar, I need you to get going on those deliveries."

"Yes, Mr. Evans."

"And take Tom with you. I'd like to get him acclimated to the route."

"To the route?" thought Edgar. *"That's my territory. What the hell does Evans want me showing—wait, oh no, Evans is trying to give that blackguard my job—he expects me to train him. I won't do it."*

Edgar entertained thoughts of sabotage as he walked down the hallway to the break room. As he got closer, he could hear that brazen buffoon's excessive laughs bouncing off the Formica counters and the tabletops.

"And then the colored boy said—"

"Tom"—the room came to a standstill as Edgar entered like a wet fart in a crowded elevator—"you're to come with me. Evans put *me* in charge."

"Ha! In charge of my balls."

The room exploded with laughter—a crowd of break-room monkeys guffawing at Tom's quip.

Edgar would list them later.

He attempted to lead the way to his car, but Tom stepped before him.

"What an asshole. You really think you're something, don't you."

He took notice of the cut of Tom's slacks—the way they clung to his muscled buttocks as he peacocked his way through the corridor.

"I'll show you. We'll see who's the big man."

As they reached the interstate, Edgar laid down the law.

"These clients are important, Tom. A few of them we've had since the 80s, they're pretty much—"

Tom reached up to the visor, unfastened the vanity glass, laid it squarely on the dashboard, and then dumped the contents of a small paper bindle upon it—white powder in fine crystalline form.

"What the hell is that?" said Edgar.

"It's blow, bitch—do you want some?"

"No, I don't *want some*. And you don't want any either. What do you think you're doing?"

"I'm getting your fucking noise out of my head. It's time you shut the fuck up—and one more thing, I ain't doing shit today. This is a joy ride, as far as I'm concerned."

Edgar swallowed hard and squeezed the steering wheel.

Tom was too big to handle.

His associate rolled a hundred-dollar bill into a makeshift straw. He held it over the powder, put one end into his left nostril, and inhaled a nice long dusty cloud of coke.

"And, uh, Eddie. You're gonna have to step on it; I'm not gonna sit here while you pussy-foot the pedals."

"But what about the police?"

"Fuck the police."

Tom took another long blast, finishing the blow with his right nostril, then licking his finger and wiping the mirror.

The car accelerated.

Tom leaned back and smiled.

"How does it feel, Eddie, knowing I'm about to take your job—you are aware of that, aren't you?"

"Yes, I guess I am."

"Hmmm, I guess you are." The big man laughed as Edgar fumed.

The drive was silent for the most part—that is, if you didn't count the occasional giggle emitting from the coked-up Tom.

"Will you be coming in with me?" Edgar asked. "This owner can be a real ball-buster."

"I'll show you a ball buster. How about this, Eddie."

Tom stretched his left foot over and stomped on Edgar's shoe—trapping Edgar's foot against the gas pedal and ruthlessly accelerating the car through traffic.

"Tom! Please! Stop! Stop it, Tom!"

They careened through a red light, narrowly missing a school bus—the children's screams echoing in the rear-view mirror.

A siren came to life behind them.

"Tom, the police!"

The big man laughing, lifted his foot.

Edgar braked and pulled to the curb.

This was what he'd been waiting for. The universe had opened a door of escape, and he was going to walk right through.

"All I have to do is give Tom to the policeman—that sociopathic bully will be arrested and fired for sure."

Tom reached into his jacket, extracted a fat bindle, and then tucked it into Edgar's top left pocket.

"You let that ride, Eddie, and keep your fucking mouth shut."

The officer slapped the roof of Edgar's car—"You wanna roll that window down?"

"Yes, yes." Edgar stuttered as he rolled down the glass.

"What the hell were you doing back there? Have you been drinking?"

"No, of course not. I haven't been."

Edgar reached into his pocket, bravely pulled out the cocaine, and pointed at Tom.

"He gave me this. He made me hold it. He made the car go."

The officer leaned down and investigated the vehicle—his eyes hovered over Tom—a quick smile followed.

"Is that right?" he said, turning back to Edgar. "License and registration, please." Edgar pulled the door handle, the officer kicked it shut with his knee—"and stay in the car—nobody told you to get out...yet."

As the officer walked back to his cruiser, Tom reached into his pants pocket, pulled out a mini bottle of Cutty Sark, took a quick sip, then sprinkled the remaining contents over Edgar—liberally dousing his crotch.

"What the hell, Tom?"

"You can't hold your booze, Sissy."

The officer walked back to Edgar's vehicle and asked him to exit. Tom followed suit, climbing from the car. He addressed the policeman.

"How's it going there, Bud?"

"Oh, really good, Tom. Are you still attending that AA meeting at the church?"

"You bet. Clean and sober six months."

Tom held up an AA key tag and nodded towards the stunned Edgar.

"I've been trying to straighten this one out but, oh well."

The officer put a hand on Edgar's shoulder and pushed him against the car.

He brought out his cuffs and secured the poor man.

"But I didn't—" Edgar pleaded—"It's him, he did it."

"Denial," Tom said. "It's not just a river in Egypt, Edgar."

He wiped a bit of powder off his nostril.

"But don't worry, I'll finish up the route and tell Evans you were...*delayed*."

He nodded toward Edgar's car.

"Are the keys in it?"

Edgar—the bitch—politely nodded his head.

The Visitor

She was slumped in the passenger seat—the car idling—pop tunes playing on the radio. I stood outside wondering if she was breathing.

I couldn't sleep, so I'd come out of my house to have a smoke, when I'd noticed the car.

It was your standard chick mobile—Volkswagen convertible, light blue with a soft grey top—the kind of car mommy and daddy thought she'd look cute in.

I knocked on the glass. No answer.

I knocked again—this time a bit harder. Not desperate or worried in any way—just harder.

She slightly moved her head.

She was a blonde—or at least her hair was. Through the window, that tangled mass looked as if it'd seen a bottle or two of Speed-Lite, but who was I to judge?

I've fried my hair a thousand times—as we speak, it's a nice shade of Passion Pink.

I knocked again.

This time she turned toward the glass, spit out a mouthful of her curls, and looked up at me with Alice Cooper eyes—the result of cheap mascara coursing down her cheeks.

Tears have a way of breaking down even the strongest of eye paint—she'd been crying.

"Are you okay?" I asked.

She sat up—sheepishly smiled at the wolf outside her door, and then she quick-fluffed her way into what she thought was presentable. She turned off the car and rolled down the window.

"Hey," she said—not a care in the world. "What's up?"

"What's up? Are you fucking kidding me? You're sitting out here looking like what's half dead and you *what-up* me? Are you okay?"

"Yeah," she said—slowly coming together. "I was just resting—waiting, I guess."

"You want me to call someone?"

"No, I already did. He's right here."

It was then that I heard it—a tight transistor voice coming out of the cellphone lying on the driver's seat.

"Cindy," the voice called. "Who the fuck is that? What are you doing?"

She looked over at the phone and then back to me.

"He's a cheating prick. This is payback."

She opened the car door, swung around, and casually spread her legs.

"Kat told me where you live"—she wasn't wearing panties—"Do you want me?"

I took a hit off my cigarette and hunched down before her. I blew a cloud of smoke across her fishnets. I've always found despair and vengeance attractive.

I reached out and slid my hand between her hair and neck—gently squeezed and pulled her toward me. I placed a light kiss upon her forehead.

She was a young woman carelessly scorned.

"Cindy!"

The man's voice on the phone was frantic, feeling the gravity of what he'd done.

I kissed her again—this time on the lips. She tasted sweet—a boozy nectar of pain and tears.

I reached over her and picked up the phone.

"Hang on a minute—what's your name, sweetheart?"

"I'm Eric. Who's this—"

"Not you, her."

"Her name's Cindy. She's my girlfriend—who the fuck is this?"

I smiled at the girl.

"Do you wanna come inside or do it here?"

She leaned forward and pulled down my sweatpants. I wasn't wearing britches.

She had a talented mouth—took pride in her work.

I turned my attention to the phone.

"Yeah, she may not be the forgiving type, but fuck, guy—that's quite a mouth on her, yeah? You must be some sort of playboy to blow off a girl like this."

"Who is this?"

"I'm a friend of Mindy's... I mean Cindy's—she's not happy with you."

"Let me talk to her, please. I'm sorry."

"Well, she can't speak right now—hold up, less teeth, more spit, sweetheart—but if you hang tight a minute, I'll set you up."

I pulled away from the girl and extended my hand. She took it and exited the car.

As she stood, I pulled her close and kissed her.

I accidentally dropped the phone in the gutter.

To her luck it was dry.

The voice on the other end was still clear. I picked it up and handed it to her. She held it to her ear as I lifted her onto the hood of her car.

I spread her legs as she said hello.

"Fuck, you, Eric. I hope she was worth it."

I couldn't hear his reply, but as I pushed into her, she moaned and pulled the phone slightly away from her ear.

There he was—*"Please, Baby, don't!"*

I've never understood these guys.

They go out on their girls, grab a bit of strange, and they've got no problem with it whatsoever. But when their lady finds out, and she gives them the same in kind, they act as if it's the end of the world—like their sweet flower has cast a mortal sin upon their hearts.

I think it must be immaturity.

When I was younger, I felt the same, but as I got older—and knew I was incapable of being faithful—I got used to it, and even came to enjoy it.

I took the phone out of her hand.

"How old are you buddy?"

"I'm 23."

"And Cindy, how old is she?"

"Who the fuck is this?"

I was about to cum.

"Hey, sweetheart, are you okay to drive or should he come get you?"

She wrapped a leg around me as she moaned her reply.

She was good to go.

I returned my attention to the phone.

"Okay, here's what's gonna happen. I'm gonna finish up here—make sure she's satisfied—and then I'm gonna get mine.

"She says she's good to drive, so after she gets herself together, I'll have her drive over to your place.

"And you better be nice to her this time—keep your dick in your pants. And remember, she knows where I live—and seems to be enjoying herself.

"So, when she gets there, draw a nice bath for her—after all, this is your fault."

I returned the phone to Cindy as I finished up.

Is There a Hypnotist Onboard?

"We've just reached 10,000 ft.—you may now switch on your approved electronic devices. We should have a smooth flight and be arriving in Oakland in about 50 minutes."

I don't know if you ever saw those comic books—the old pulp type where they had adverts in the back. You know what I'm talking about—*draw this pirate to see if you have artistic talent, 1,000 Sea Monkeys for a dollar*, and *how-to pick-up chicks through hypnosis*. That last one was my favorite. I was a young boy dying to see what a real titty looked like. I had ragged old copies of Playboy, but I wanted the real thing.

I sent away for the instruction manual. When it arrived, I thought I was a few pages away from getting a look down Ms. O'Conner's top—the unattached mother of two who lived next door with her great big tits. But that book did nothing for me. It was just a bunch of flim-flam bullshit that didn't work—you can believe me, I tried. I got an ass-whipping for telling Ms. O that she was under my spell and to remove her pants.

Yeah, the book was a joke, but it started me off on a path to learn the real thing—hypnosis—not that stage shit either. I'm talking about clinical hypnosis and the ability to plant suggestions into people's heads through calming chatter that's meant to relax and enlighten. It turned out I was great at it—a natural. A Master Hypnotherapist is what they call me these days.

I smile at the woman next to me—early thirties, cute in a *hey-she's-right here* kind of way. I notice the inexpensive Tar-jay outfit and a ring finger with a slug-white band of untanned skin where the ring used to be—a recent divorcee. She's clutching a book against her chest—*Women Who Love Too Much*—I'm familiar with it. My ex-wife had a copy.

I take a quick assessment. She's only one or two steps below a contender—a slightly too large nose and a matching breast job drop her down to undercard status, but I'm interested. She looks like she's still hurting over a marriage that was supposed to last forever but got KO'd in the first round. She could use a quick boost.

I begin the conversation.

"I like these short flights. Even if it's bumpy, it's over quick, and you can move on."

"Yes, I guess so."

You see what I did there? A short flight—in regard to her marriage. She was young and couldn't have been hitched long. A bumpy ride—the arguments, the hostilities between the two of them. And then, I basically reached inside her subconscious mind, buoyed her acceptance of the relationship being kaput, and gave her the okay to put herself back on the market.

32

"My wife used to say—when she wasn't cheating on me—that she loved the rough flights. The 600-mph struggle of air and plane conflict. As expected, she brought the same love of drama into our relationship. I was unwilling to chalk up her frequent flier miles. I sent her packing."

Boom—did you hear that, subconscious? Here's a man who doesn't want to waste time arguing, and cheating isn't acceptable. He knows what he wants, and he stands up for what he believes in.

I watched her eyes sail over me. I was wearing a charcoal-grey suit with a white button-down shirt. Even without a tie, I looked professional.

"Are you a therapist?" she asked.

I smiled without answering—*implying my credentials, which in reality are non-existent.*

"Loyalty and love are traits that some of us have, and hopefully the object of our affection is up to the challenge when we bestow those traits upon them. Wouldn't you agree? You were up to the challenge, weren't you?"

"Yes, I was."

"And you wanted a partner that was worthy of your love."

"Yes, I did—I do."

"Do you have children—uh...?"

"Daphne—and no, I don't."

"Ahhh, to be unencumbered by baggage. To be free to love and to give yourself as you've always wished... Daphne—such a beautiful name."

She smiled and sat tall in her chair. The plane rolled slightly. I lightly squeezed her arm and then released.

"I bet you like the ocean."

"I do. I love it."

"I can believe that..."

"What do you mean by that? How can you tell?"

"Well, you portray grace—strength—as if you could pass through a great storm and remain fluid, almost stronger from the conflict. And also, your name... sometimes, subconsciously, we take on the etymology of our names. Daphne—a Greek Nymph. A water spirit."

I stopped speaking, picked up an inflight magazine, thumbed to a random page, and began to read.

Disinterest should be illegal. It works every time—butter the bread, but don't eat it.

"Are you done with me?" she said, "I was enjoying our conversation."

I closed the magazine, yet still held it in my hand.

"I didn't want you to feel as if you were being pursued. I could imagine a woman like yourself is often the... I don't want to say target, that's not right"—*I looked her over. She watched as my eyes took her in. It was only natural that she would want to be approved of*—"Hmmm, something loftier. Let's just say that I could imagine many men would consider you the apex of their desire."

I slightly changed my vocal tone as I said the words: I, you, and desire—practically undetectable to the listener, and yet, the mind inside her gathered those words and her subconscious was not displeased.

She laughed—her posture relaxed, her arms open, her hope returned.

"What about you," she said, "what's the uh... apex of your desire?"

"That's sweet of you to ask, but you don't have to."

"No seriously." She leaned toward me to prove her interest.

At least that's what it would look like to the casual observer, but to me—the master—I'd hooked her inner-self and I was reeling her in.

"Tell me" she pleaded. "What do you desire in a woman?"

I looked deep into her eyes, held her gaze before I spoke.

"I want a woman that's been burned. A woman that's had the worst, so she can recognize and be grateful for the best. I want a woman who loves herself and is unwilling to settle for anything less. Isn't that what you want, Daphne? Don't you want to be loved like that?"

That night, as I fucked her, I thought about being a kid. I thought about Ms. O'Connor and that great set of tits. If I was gonna say anything to the young men of today—I'd suggest hypnosis and my latest book, "*How-to Pick-up Chicks.*"

The Beat-down

"You don't know what I deal with—the human waste that I wade through. I can't sleep. It's killing me, Laura."

"Oh, fuck you—it's always *you*. What about us; what about your son? He used to be proud of you, and now I hear him laugh when he tells his friends what you do."

He buttoned his shirt—dark blue over white 'T' and a protective vest. He checked his service revolver and picked up his keys.

"Maybe you should think about living somewhere else until you get a grip on your head. You need to see somebody, Frank. I don't know who, but I'm done."

He took her words like he took the world—like it couldn't hurt him if he ignored it. But the stench of the world shadowed him, and her words beat him to the car—a black and white, waiting in the driveway. His 454 chariot of despair.

The first call was a 415, which rolled into a domestic violence beef—a couple of tweakers arguing over nothing. A haggard old—

maybe young—woman crying about some bitch named Crystal who'd taken something and fucked her old man.

Frank looked the 'old man' over—motherfucker had more fingers than teeth. The scars on his face—deep oozing craters—outnumbered the cars on the highway. Pestilence walking.

He tried to listen—to make sense of the mess—but his attention kept drifting to a small boy in filthy clothes. Kid was too old to be sucking his thumb He stood near the wall, bouncing his head off the plaster.

"Hey, cop! Are you listening, man?"

"Yeah, I'm listening. Here's the deal: if you tell me she hit you, she goes with me. But I'm looking at those red marks on her neck, and she says you choked her. So you both go. And the boy"—Frank nodded at the kid—"he goes to CPS. What'll it be?"

"I want him to stop fucking her!"

Frank pulled out his cuffs. "Okay, fuck it."

The old skeleton who'd been sport-fucking Crystal and choking the girl grabbed her by the arm. "I'm sorry officer. We'll work it out, okay?"

"Okay then,"—he replaced his cuffs—"clean up the kid. Get him something to eat."

As the night dragged on, it got worse.

There was a stabbing at 6th and Rose—some border-brother had cut up a kid over a few bucks and a bicycle. Two inches lower and the knife would've broken on a belt buckle. Instead, just another nameless fuck bleeding out in a gutter. They loaded him into the ambulance. His mother showed. Frank tried to comfort her, but when her son died on the gurney, she was past consolation.

By 3am Frank had cleared two more assaults, an armed robbery, and a lewd conduct involving a 47-year-old man and his 8-year-old stepdaughter.

At 4 a.m., dispatch sent him to a possible 502 /PC148(a)—drunk driver, resisting.

When he rolled on scene, the drunk was outside his car arguing with Officer Collins. Frank knew her—she was alright, good in a pinch—but this guy had a hundred pounds on her and wasn't backing down.

Frank parked his cruiser in front of the perp's car, blocking him in—taking the automotive weapon out of play.

The drunk was loud—aggressive. Frank stepped out with his baton.

A few passersby stopped to watch.

"Lie face down on the ground," Frank said—firm. No bullshit.

The drunk turned, eyes trying to focus. He smiled. "I'm gonna need ` you to—FUCK OFF, officer!"

Collins stepped to the side.

"I said, lie down!" Frank repeated. "Now!"

The drunk staggered forward. Collins moved behind.

"Lie down. Face to the ground!"

He refused.

Collins closed in.

The drunk sensed her presence. He uncoiled and swung behind him—a nose pummeling hammer fist that sent Collins to the ground.

Frank brought his baton down on the drunk's head—the skull cracked, blood rising in a vicious wave. Still, he didn't drop. He stared at Frank, unfazed, as thin torrents of alcohol-laced blood ran down his face.

"Fucking faggots"—the drunk heel-stomped the dazed Collins.

Frank swung again.

The blow grazed the drunk's jaw—no damage done. He reached for Frank—both arms extended—a monster imitating horror with inebriated precision.

Frank stepped back and kicked him in the balls—steel-toed boot, hard and low.

The drunk fell to his knees.

"Lay down!" Frank screamed. The man refused to comply. "Lay down—face down on the ground!"

The drunk raised his head—and as he faced Frank, a movie of the officer's life played in his eyes. A child raped. A boy murdered. A tidal wave of violence and despair projected by his gaze.

He moaned, and the soundtrack to Frank's depression—his failures and futility—echoed harsh into the night. The stench of the world rose like street corner piss on his breath.

Frank choked back the stink—swallowed the bile.

I am a man against the tide. I am alone.

He could feel the hurt rising from his gut—*a man can only take so much.*

Collins rose and steadied herself.

She'd be alright—she had this.

"Lay down—"

The drunk finally descended, palms to the pavement—inhaling and exhaling the dust of the street.

I am honor, and code, order, and justice. He is an insult to the promise of humanity.

For a moment, Frank held.

Then, as his mouth filled with the virulence of the world, Frank unholstered his revolver and dispatched 502 slash pc148a—four in the back, one to the head—before retching and turning the gun on himself.

The Suit

It was long enough in the arms and just right at the crotch. He'd worried it might be too constricting, but when he pulled on the head, it was pleasantly airy. He admired himself in the mirror.

"Oh my. I am a grand beast."

He ruffled his cloth feathers and stuck out his chest.

"Bok, bok, bok. Cock-a-doodle-doo!"

The suit was magnificent. He hoped Stella would love it as much as he did. He strutted around the room, clucking and boking, knocking into furniture and, without regard, breaking a very expensive vase—a gift from Stella's mother. He was reckless and wild, a real beast.

He was also out $800—the cost of the size-42 chicken suit.

The phone rang.

"Harry?" It was Stella.

"Yes, dear?"

"Why is your voice muffled?"

He tried to speak clearly, but the slit in the beak wasn't made for human speech.

"I'm not sure, Baby, I—bok!"

"Don't 'Baby' me. I just tried to buy a pair of work shoes and our card was declined. They said we made an $800 purchase—Barbie's Pleasure Palace. Did you buy something?"

Harry cocked his head to one side. He scratched the carpet with his right foot.

"I'm not sure, dear."

"You're not sure what? Look, Harry, I'm trying. I'm really trying. My mother begged me to leave you, but I stayed. You gotta do your part, Baby. You've gotta straighten up."

"I am straight, dear. I swear it—bok!"

"And Harry?"

"Yes?"

"She's coming to dinner."

"Who?"

"My mother. She's coming for dinner."

Click.

The doorbell rang.

Harry pulled at the headpiece. It was stuck.

The doorbell rang again.

"Just a minute!"

"Harry?" It was his mother-in-law. "Let me in, I have to use the ladies room."

Harry darted about the apartment. Frantically, he fought to remove the chicken head, but it wouldn't budge.

"Bok, bok, bok," he clucked.

"Harry! What's going on in there? Let me in."

He flapped his arms and jumped onto the couch—stretched his neck and crowed.

"Bok! Cluck, cluck, cluck, bok!"

The door handle shook.

"Harry! Open the Goddamn door!"

He dashed to the piano and pecked out a tune with his plastic beak.

Nothing would dislodge the head.

"Harry! Open the fucking door!"

"Bok, bok, bok!"

The sounds of the street—seven stories below—clawed their way through the open living room window.

The city noise called to him.

"Bok, bok, bok!" he answered.

He crouched and hopped onto the sash.

"Harry! That's it, Goddamn it! I'm leaving."

It was too late. The threat was removed.

But the chicken couldn't be stilled.

I have wings and I can fly.

Harry leapt.

He flapped his arms as he fell—a great yellow ball of cloth feathers tumbling through the air.

Down, down, down—first this way, then that—almost flying, until...

Bang!

He slammed, rooster proud, onto the roof of a cab.

Harry, the chicken, was dead.

P.N.P

"Hmmm, maybe I'll have Asian tonight"—he smirked as he clicked his way through the personal ads on the casual encounters site. Women for men—although he had looked elsewhere, and more than once.

"Here's one: sweet-hearted girl—cum over and unload. Ha! She sounds sincere, but not quite what I'm looking for."

He was in his mid-thirties, had a decent job, and was technically in a committed relationship—although it was complicated.

"Ahhh, here we go—just the thing for a Tuesday afternoon. 'A caramel, big-bodied woman with favors, seeking a well-hung, generous gent—let's PNP.' Now, that's my kind of fun!"

He *was* hung—not exactly generous—but partying and playing was right up his alley. Richard enjoyed the snow, and he loved the pussy. He prepared an email detailing his specs. They might not have been spot-on—he claimed 9.5, when in reality, he was a touch short of 7—but he did include a face pic. Face shots tell people you mean business.

Amateurs attach blurry, high-angle cock pics to pump up their lack of junk. Pros know how to get it on. Richard was no amateur.

The reply email was almost instantaneous. After a few back-and-forths, they agreed to meet at a cheap motel on Harbor Blvd—the Ease-up Inn. Richard knew the place. It was a bit sketchy, but sketchy could be good. It added to the overall naughtiness of the date.

He sent a text to his girlfriend: *How 'bout dinner? I've got a meeting with the boss, and then I'm out. Wish me luck.*

He knew she'd buy it. If you're going to lie, lie first. Don't wait until they're looking for you. Make a preemptive strike, then blame them if they wonder where you've been.

He knocked lightly on the motel door—number 6, close to the icemaker and the pool. It was, as promised in the email, unlocked.

The room was as dark as cheap motels allowed—a misty twilight haze hanging heavy. Richard strolled into the scent of jungle—human breeding stink coating the air with its thick, musty odor.

The voice that greeted him was raspy—a rough, alcohol-fueled slur.

"Shut the door, Baby."

He was immediately erect.

"Let mama get a taste of you."

Richard undid his pants and stepped nearer the bed. She was big—bigger than promised—but he liked that. She pulled him close.

"That's it, baby," she said. "Hold it out for me."

Pow!

The first blow caught Richard in the mouth. The second, third, and fourth came in a rapid-fire procession. He spastically cartwheeled over the bed.

"Get that motherfucker!"

Richard threw his hands over his face—tried to cover.

"Fucking cracker bitch."

The punch exploded bright blue stars in the dark.

When he awoke, the room was empty.

He could taste blood in his mouth.

His right eye was swollen shut.

He fumbled along the wall until he found a switch—the bathroom light.

He checked himself in the mirror. He was a mess. They'd done a number on him. One of his front teeth was loose.

He reached behind him—gingerly touched his ass—blood and semen.

He wiped himself on a rough towel and staggered out of the bathroom.

His clothes were scattered. His wallet, keys, and watch—gone.

The $400 he had in his pocket. The plastic. The new phone—likewise.

He dressed and sat on the edge of the bed, held his head in his hands.

"Fucking PNP, man."

"Sometimes you party.

"Sometimes you pay."

The Believer

God's will is a strange thing—he walked down the row of shops, trying each door as he passed—*I've heard some say that if it's easy, God has a hand in it.*

He tried the door to McCluskey's parlor—a men's shop. It was unlocked.

I think I agree.

He turned the knob and entered.

However, sometimes things are difficult, and I couldn't imagine the great Czar of the Heavens wanting me to give up just because the going got hard.

The cash register drawer was open, displaying to the city streets that there was nothing here to be had.

Arlo bowed his head in prayer.

"Oh Heavenly Father, I come to you as a seeker. Please bless my hands. Deliver unto me that which I deserve."

He was guided to a dark space below the register—a hidden shelf of sorts—and he placed his hand upon a small metal cash box with an open padlock meant to secure the lid. Whoever had put the box away had been errant in making sure the lock had clicked.

"Ahhh, good old McCluskey—a special prayer I say for you, sir."

He opened the box and extracted the contents. There was a small handful of bills, some twenties, some tens—nothing larger, but a nice little score. A few hundred dollars that Arlo placed in his pocket.

He replaced the box—clicking the lock shut as it should have been done before—then turned and walked toward the door.

A flash of cool steel caught his eye. A straight razor lying open on the counter—the blade bending the streetlight's glow.

Arlo was moved to touch it—an unseen, divine force was upon him.

He picked up the razor and flashed it above. It felt good in his hand.

There was a mirror running the length of the shop. Arlo admired his reflection in it. He was neither tall nor short, his hair was dark-brown peppered with grey, and other than a long scar running from left eye to chin, he was an unremarkable man—a random sheep in God's flock.

"Do I please you, Lord?" he asked the mirror. "Because if you felt I didn't—" He violently grabbed his own hair and pulled his neck back, exposing his throat, and held the razor against it.

"I would remove thee. I would pluck this errant member from thy world, if you so command."

Arlo waited for an answer that did not come.

A car slowly drove by the shop, its headlights momentarily freezing the encounter inside.

"As you will, my Lord."

Arlo let go of his hair and dropped the razor to his side. He closed the blade and placed it in his pocket.

He took a quick glance around the shop—made sure nothing but the razor was out of place—then wiped his hands.

McCluskey would think the cashbox's contents had mysteriously vanished in the night.

It's a miracle!

Arlo giggled and locked the door on his way out.

"For this bounty, I thank you, Lord. May I always be worthy."

The street was empty as Arlo made his way to the Tavern on 4th.

He wasn't a drinking man, but the odd shot of whiskey on a cool night was more medicinal than pleasurable. *The Lord loves a sober soldier.*

Arlo pulled his jacket collar up and put his hands in his pockets. He could feel the razor riding heavy against the cloth—an unnatural weight diverting his attention from the street.

"You got a light, man?"

Arlo looked up and into the eyes of a young man. He was blond with wavy, greased back hair. A cigarette hung from his lip, and a single teardrop was tattooed beneath his right eye.

"Or some change?"

The smoker had a friend. He came alongside Arlo—not too close, but close enough.

"You gotta have change, old man."

"I don't smoke," said Arlo.

"I guess you don't do money either, huh?"

"No, I have money. I took it from the shop on the corner—look."

Arlo reached into his left pants pocket and pulled out the bills. The razor in his right rode silent and true.

"Here." He held out the cash. "It must be for you. I received it, and now I will share my bounty with those in need. The Lord does do strange works."

The blond grabbed the bills.

"What else you got, man?"

"What else?" Arlo asked.

"In your fucking pockets. What else you got?"

"I have a straight razor."

"Motherfucker."

The blond's companion shoved Arlo.

"You think you're bad man? You gonna cut us?"

"No. I'm not bad. I'm good. I'm a godly man."

Arlo reached into his right pocket and pulled forth the razor.

The handle melded to his flesh—a blade from most high given unto a trusted servant.

It opened of its own volition.

He obediently flourished the steel.

"I gave you boys what was asked," he said, "and now you want more?"

The two men circled.

Arlo prayed.

"Father, shelter me, your humble son."

The would-be robbers laughed.

"Give to me the power of your hands—the strength of your will."

The blond made his move. But as he attacked, he slipped—the heels of his black steel-toed boots finding no purchase on the pavement. He fell to his knees.

Arlo, with a knowing smile, wrapped his hand in the blond's hair, pulling the man's head back, exposing his throat.

"Thank you, Father. For this I offer you."

A slight wave of the blade and the skin parted wide—a red sea of blood cascaded to the now sanctified ground.

Arlo released the blond's hair. The body fell in posture supplicant.

"It is the fate of all men to die."

Arlo turned toward the companion.

Unseen hands secured the struggling thief.

God held him in place.

Arlo advanced.

"I'm thirsty, Father," Arlo said, "and I'm tired. Lord, hear my plea."

"I hear you, my son."

Magically, the man's head snapped back, exposing his throat.

Arlo held the blade against the street thief's neck.

"Do this for me, Arlo. Please me, and a cold beer awaits."

His God was a good God.

A God of justice and mercy and...

He slit the man's throat.

...honor.

The Geek

The Geek had pissed himself.

Passed out in the corner.

There was a fresh yellow puddle on the floor that was not beer.

His handler kicked him in the ribs.

"Let's go, Master. You got ten minutes."

The Geek lifted his head and smiled with swollen lips.

Dressed in torn blue-jeans cuffed over workman's boots, a ripped New York Dolls T-shirt, three leather belts wrapped around his waist, and an old leather jacket with the word, *Chaos* stenciled on the back in white spray paint.

His leather cap, he'd cocked to one side on his balding head.

He resembled a mid-November jack-o'-lantern—a few broken teeth and a fake gold crown with a zirconia glistening in the dim light.

"I need another beer," he slurred. "I know we got a fucking tab. That fucking kike needs to get his shit right."

"He'll get right," his handler said. "Just get up. I'll get you one."

He rose, bones cracking and popping beneath mottled white skin.

A warm, open can of lukewarm suds was placed in his hand.

"It's show time fuckers. Let's rock and roll!"

The club was small—room for a hundred if they would have shown. But tonight was a light house; fifty or sixty aging old punks hoping to catch a look at the Master of Three Chord Disaster.

Drunken catcalls and jeers followed as he staggered towards the stage like a spastic Elvis with a twice busted hip.

He puked as he wrapped his hand around the microphone.

The small crowd cheered.

He backhanded two fingers to the audience.

It was the British equivalent of *fuck you*, but the geek was from Hollywood and had never been overseas.

"Okay, fuckers," he called in a loose Cockney snarl. "'Ere' we go now!"

His backing band cranked into gear, and the old punks circled round the stage.

They bumped and swayed and creaked and groaned.

"I ain't no corporate stooge," the Geek howled. "I ain't no government boy. I'm as right as a free man can be. I ain't no victim of Miss Liberty."

After a sloppy forty-five-minute set the band dropped their instruments and called it a night.

The crowd returned to the bar.

The Geek made his way backstage and sat—sober as he'd been in years.

It was one of those rare nights when his alcoholic haze remained as sweat on the stage.

He ran his hand down his arm.

Tattoos of sailing scenes passed under his fingers.

He'd never been to sea.

A mist of clarity rose as he belched.

"Do you think I'm a joke?" the Geek asked. "Am I valid?"

The handler counted out his percentage of a small take.

"You're punk as fuck, buddy—you ain't no corporate stooge."

"No," the Geek was ready for another beer.

"I sure as fuck ain't no stooge."

Community—Okay?

It looked like something that had fallen off the back of a truck.

But when I got closer, I could see that it was an old man on his knees in the street.

I stopped my car and helped him to his feet. His pant leg was torn—there was some blood—not much, but it would need to be tended to. I walked him to my car and had him lean against the hood.

He'd been carrying groceries. The brown paper bag he was toting had ripped, and his canned goods and a few heads of lettuce had rolled away. His milk—escaping a torn carton—had made its way into the gutter.

"Your bag is trashed, Pops."

I opened my trunk and pulled out a cloth carry-all. I have a hundred of them. Every time I go to the market, I forget to bring my own, so I buy a new one.

I collected what groceries were savable.

"I usually get paper," he said. "It's cheaper."

A car honked as they came upon us—entitled cunts thinking they own the street. It's a residential neighborhood, and we have a situation, big fucking deal—we're residents.

I hate what they've done to this place. The whole small-town beach vibe has been replaced with ugly three-story cookie-cutter monoliths populated with assholes like this—no respect for community.

"Fuck you," I said as they passed.

I smiled at the old man. "Sorry."

He raised his arm and flashed an old middle finger at the rear window of the Tesla as they silently pulled away.

"Yeah, fuck 'em."

He returned my smile.

I offered him a ride home, which he accepted.

Along the way, we stopped at the corner market. I had him wait in the car as I went in. I replaced his milk and lettuce, bought him a dark candy bar and hid it in the bag, grabbed a package of wipes, some Band-Aids, and a tube of that antibiotic shit.

"Hey, *hombre*. You doing the lottery today? You look very lucky."

"Fuck you, Angel, you know I swore off that shit."

The clerk laughed as he handed me my change.

I returned to the car. The old man was holding my son's ball glove—he held it to his face and inhaled the scent of leather and summer.

"You're the family that lives on Alabama—the ones with the kids jumping and yelling?"

"Yeah, sorry, they uh… "

"No," he said, "I like it. I had kids. I don't see them anymore. My boy passed a few years ago, and Jenny, my little girl, a few years before him.

"Sometimes, I sit in the backyard and listen to yours while I think about mine…"

He closed his eyes and lay back against the seat.

"My Margrett—she's gone too."

"I have five," I said. "Two boys and three girls. I couldn't imagine losing them."

"Oh, you don't ever lose them. You miss holding them, but they're never really gone."

I drove him to an old single-story Craftsman, bordered on each side by soulless, two-million-dollar boxes.

"They want my place—offered me quite a penny for it. But I'm not ready to have my memories torn down. They can take it when I'm gone."

I got out of the car, opened his door, and helped him out.

"Do you think I could come by some day?" he said. "Watch the kids play?"

"Yeah, of course, we'd love it—but no fireworks. And if you break something, you've gotta fix it—those are the rules."

I carried his groceries to his door.

"I put a little treat in there for you," I said, "but you gotta take care of that leg first."

I shook his hand—his grip was strong, a working man's grasp.

He looked me eye to eye—clear, bright, kindly.

"You know what, you look like a crafty old prick, how 'bout we come get you?"

"Ha! You'd better."

He tapped the side of his nose as he went inside.

An After Christmas Tale

It was his usual *Holy-Night* pitch, and he delivered it with the proper mixture of warmth, warning, and wisdom. A Christmas tale complete with angels and wise men, a virgin birth, and a miracle child.

His hair was perfect, his teeth sparkling white. He was in his mid-40s, faithfully married to a loving wife. He was a strong man, father to two beautiful boys. He was generous, loving, and kind—beyond reproach. If you could find fault, you could say that he was, at times, burdened by pride, but his congregation felt blessed by his presence. And when he finished speaking and shaking hands—graciously accepting their praise—he kissed his wife and children goodbye, told them he would be along soon, and then he walked to his car.

It's strange how things happen, he thought, *how God works wonders in the world.*

He unlocked the door of his mid-sized sedan, climbed in, put on his seat belt, and then reached for the .38 caliber revolver in the glovebox. The gun was one of God's blessings—a weapon taken from the hand of a jealous parishioner. It was to be an instrument of rage and revenge, but now, thanks to his intercession, it would be used as something entirely different.

He watched as the headlights of his flock faded away, drifting like snow flurries toward their homes. He checked to make sure the gun was loaded and then he began to sing.

Have yourself a merry little Christmas—let your heart be light. From now on, our troubles will be out of sight.

"Hey, Tony, are you okay?"

He looked up and into the eyes of Albert, the caretaker of the church—the one he'd been waiting for.

"Yeah, I'm all right," the pastor replied. "I was just sitting and singing and thinking."

"Buddy, you've got a gun there. Are you sure?"

He covered the revolver with his hand.

"It's just that... this time of year is a time of love and family—hope and promise—but if you don't have those things, or if they're being taken from you, then this time of year is a time that magnifies loss. It's a season of pain and betrayal. A time of failure. Of a job not well done..."

He lifted the gun.

"Hey, come on, Tony, put it down, huh? You don't have to do this." Albert opened the door and put his hand on the pastor's shoulder—"I just heard you in there—it was beautiful..."

"Was my son beautiful when you touched him? Did you tell yourself that you didn't have to do this?"

"What? Come on, man. What the fuck are you talking about?"

"I'm talking about you molesting my boy."

"Hey, what the fuck—don't shoot me, man. I got kids, please."

"I'm not going to shoot you—you're not the one who failed. I did. You're a sinner, you do what sinners do.

"I forgive you."

Tony—no longer the pastor—put the gun into his mouth and pulled the trigger.

Carol

I noticed that his coffee hadn't been touched. His head was down—visibly sweating over a black leather book.

He was oblivious to the world—a perfect target.

A creepy self-help guru once said, *"We must comfort the disturbed and disturb the comfortable."*

I leave the comfortable alone and disturb the disturbed.

I opened with something harmless but intruding.

"It's a great day, isn't it?"

He looked up at me with eyes echoing a deep longing or despair—a look I knew well. Whatever he had been pondering had taken him far from this place.

"Yes," he replied. "Carol loved days like this—perfect days, she said—cinnamon and apple spice, wool sweaters, and fire-lit evenings..."

He stroked the book as he talked, almost as if he were caressing the soft back of a lover.

"Late fall was always her favorite."

I sat beside him.

"Is Carol your wife?"

"No. She lived next door."

Again, to the book his hand traveled—this time placing his fingers under the worn cover, slightly lifting.

"I bet she's at the park; she loves to walk."

He opened to the first page, and there—a photo, taken from some distance, of a woman walking her dog. A Boston terrier that looked a touch overfed.

"She was wonderful with him—very kind, loving."

"You talk as if she's gone. Did she pass?"

"No!" He clenched his hands. The blood chased from his flesh. "Of course not!"

He took a deep-sea breath.

"It's just that I'm...well...I'm not supposed to see her—it's complicated and a bit unfair."

He turned another page. This time a photo—taken from behind, of a woman walking upstairs. Then another of her in a grocery store. Then a high-angle shot of her lying topless in a yard—he smirked at that last one.

Each photo was candid. The subject unaware.

"So... are you restrained?"

"I wouldn't call this restrained"—he held up his book—"but there are certain parameters that I must abide..."

"Like three hundred yards and no phone calls?"

"Exactly."

I leaned over and gently touched his prize—toying with him. I opened it to a random page. He didn't resist.

"I wonder where she is now. Who she's with. What she has on."

He leaned back and closed his eyes, crying meekly—solemn tears searching for her on his face.

"I bet it's a real bitch not having her."

It was then that I looked down. The page I picked—not a random shot from far away, a sneak taken unawares—but a close-up. An intimate portrait of the most beautiful woman I'd ever seen.

Her eyes held the light of a thousand torches, the paper page struggling—and failing—to contain their heat. I could taste her. Feel her. She was a woman created by God to soothe every hurt, right every wrong—she was mine.

The needle tore my skin as it plunged. I looked to him, ready to battle for possession of the book—possession of her—but there would be no fight. In his eyes, only relief.

"She's yours now," he said. "I hope you enjoy her as much as I did. She really is quite wonderful—but then again, you know that now, don't you?"

There was comfort in his step as he walked away. He was lighter—free. He'd left the leather-bound book on the table.

It was heavier than I thought. I gingerly stroked its spine, held its skin against mine, inhaled the promise of its pages.

I opened it.

An address and name, scrawled in delicate hand, begged my consideration:

Carol, 184 S. Lombard St.

A Cold Reading

I could tell you that I read minds, but that's not exactly true. It's not like you could think of a color and I'd name it—I'm not a long-shot carny guesser. But let's say you were having an *emotional involvement* with a color—I could read that. And it wouldn't be by some dark swami magic. I read your body—an advertisement we humans broadcast daily, without even knowing.

All of us read people—maybe not consciously, but when we see someone grimace, or smile, or bite their lip, we infer the emotions behind those gestures. It's basic unspoken human communication. But one can go further.

We live in a selfish society—a warped civilization of self-absorbed children. Most of us are too wrapped up in our own lives to really watch anyone else. Is the person we're looking at leaning forward or back? Are they neutral or carrying tension? Are their lips tight? Eyes squinted or wide? Is their brow pinched and furrowed, relaxed, or Botox-stretched smooth? And what of their hands—at rest? Or white knuckled, gripped tight?

The human body is a ticker tape of movement—transmitting emotional information and begging to be read. There are no secrets in a world of human connection. As long as you're willing to step out of yourself and actually be a partner in the transaction of communication, you can make a shitload of money.

I learned how to read people the way a child learns to read a book. I started with a few basic combinations—frown, forward posture, tight lips—which, by the way, translates to: *unpleasant task ahead, will be met with aggressive fortitude.* Then I expanded into greater complexities. I built a human posture vocabulary until I could read *volumes* in a single gesture. And the more I studied, the clearer the communication became—until it seemed like I was reading minds.

Take this man here, for instance. "Good afternoon, sir."

"Are you addressing me?"

He wore a black suit, conservative cut. White shirt. Red power tie. Hands soft, manicured. I'm picking up a tryst—illicit romance. He reads like a wife-cheating-creep. I bet he's fucking his local nail lady.

Prepare your wallet. sir.

"Yes," I replied. "Are you still fucking that young Asian girl?"

He touched his ring finger. His eyes lifted upward and to the left—the telltale sign of constructing a lie.

"I'm sure I don't know what you're talking about," he said.

"I'm sure you do. And it'll cost you a hundred for me to walk away. Or I could just tell your wife."

I had him.

He leaned forward—engaging, intent, ready to make a deal...

Then he pulled his phone from his pocket and dialed the police.

Mommy Porn

"Hey Jack, could you write me an ad?"

"For what?"

"A personal—I'm looking for a new chick."

"What happened to the last one?"

"She was crazy."

"What are you talking about? I met her—she was great."

"Yeah, until she started getting weird."

"Weird? You're a fucking deviant. How was *she* getting weird?"

"She was reading and shit…"

"Oh, an intellectual. I can see how that might frighten you."

"No, man, she was reading *mommy porn.*"

"Like pregnant girls and stuff?"

"No, like bored housewife bondage crap—*I haven't been fucked for so long that I'm dreaming of vampire lovers and anal gaping werewolves.*"

"So what? Lots of chicks read that shit; it's not gonna kill you. Just let her tie you up a few times, and she'll get tired of it."

"No man, I dumped her. It was…bad."

"Really? Please enlighten me with your definition of *bad*."

"All right, how's this, bro? Last week she asked me if I wanted to take a *naughty drive*. So, we head out to the canyon—out by Ortega—and she got all heavy in the car. She hops in the backseat and starts playing with herself—toys and everything—really working it up."

"That's sounds terrible—I'm disgusted."

"Hold tight, fucker. I get it—there ain't nothing wrong with that, and I'm a few drinks in and down for whatever, so great. But then we pull over, and she says she wants to get out, so we do. She's wearing this super short, clingy, black dress thing—real sexy—no panties. And we're right on the side of the road. I'm thinking about doing her on the hood, when she stops me, reaches in her purse, and pulls out a pair of furry metal handcuffs.

"'Look what I got, Baby,' she says—and then she cuffs me to the door handle and pulls my fucking pants off."

"Bullshit. You had to help her."

"Yeah, of course I did—like I said, I was in but—"

"You're so full of shit."

"Fuck you. I'm not shitting you, man. I'm cuffed to the door wearing shirt and socks—nothing else. And I'm like, okay, let's do this. But then I see some headlights—and we're right on the side of the road—so I tell her, 'let me go!' but she ain't moving. She's giggling and laughing—wiggling around like it's a real thing. I'm tugging on those fucking cuffs—they looked like kid shit to me—but I can't get my ass loose. And then this fucking car pulls up and stops. The headlights right on me."

"Ha! Fuck you."

"No, I'm serious, man. Now get this—out of this car hops some big, greezy-looking, black cat—all Jheri curled up and wearing a velvet cape. He's tripping all gothic and swirly—like he's a fucking vampire or something. I'm like, 'Hey fucker, back off!' But he doesn't. He gets too close—not close enough to put a hurting on—but right there, just out of kicking range. And he's rubbing his shit. I'm fucking kicking at him, he's flapping that fucking cape, and hissing at me like he's a creature from beyond the grave. I'm like 'Fuck, you. I'll fucking kill you, dude,' but he ain't listening.

"He pulls down his fucking tights and whips out his shit—you know, a fucking black baby's arm, and he *whacks* it at me."

"What do you mean *at you?*"

"I mean, RIGHT FUCKING AT ME! He's pointing it at me as he jerks off. I'm spitting and kicking and trying to get off that fucking door handle. Look at my wrist."

He offers me a swollen hand with a huge, purple and black bruise around his wrist.

"Jesus."

"Yeah—I'm fucking telling you, dude. She ends up going down on him—gets on her knees, right out of boot range—and after he's satisfied, he flaps his cape a couple times, hops in his fucking mobile, and drives off—like nothing.

"Hey, no problem, dude, just another Saturday night at the castle, motherfucker."

"Then what?"

"Then she starts crying—saying how sorry she was, calling herself a slut, and basically kicking her own ass. I told her to let me loose, but she's scared I'm gonna hurt her, so she fucking high-tails it—runs off. I sat there for two fucking hours before the cops rolled up and uncuffed me."

"You're lucky you got out of there."

"Yeah, I'm lucky. But I'm out one chick, and I got a company barbeque to go to. So can you write me an ad?

"Wanted—no cuffs, no bats, no fooling around. Good Christian girl with morals and a car."

School Girl

She was standing near the corner of Harbor and Garden Grove Blvd. A young, brown-haired girl, nondescript, student type—looked like she was waiting for a bus.

A light rain had just begun to fall.

I felt sorry for her.

I did a U-turn and pulled up to the curb, rolled down the passenger window, and asked if she needed a ride. She smiled—she was pretty—school-girl cute.

She put her hands on the door and leaned in—ran her eyes over me and the car—a quick check, then opened the door and slid inside.

"Sure," she said, "I'd love one."

I pulled away from the curb and immediately stopped at the red light.

"Where are you going?"

She squeezed my leg—her fingernail polish was chipped and green—deep forest green.

I'm not sure why I remember that so well—the color of her nails. I think my first love's eyes were green. Maybe that's it.

"That depends on you, baby," she said. "Do you wanna get a room or are you looking for something else?"

I wasn't looking for anything. I was two months away from a divorce—still pretending to be married, and I wasn't sure where she was going with this.

"I don't do drugs. I don't drink either."

"I'm not asking you to get high," she said. "I'm asking if you want some of this"—she slid her hand across her breasts.

"I didn't know you were working, I just—"

"—Randomly pick up stray girls and get hard when they squeeze your leg? Come on, dude, get honest. You're fucking cruising and you stopped for me. Now do you wanna pull over—I know a spot behind the market—or do you wanna get a room?"

The light turned green.

I accelerated and kept my eyes on the road, but my right hand strayed onto her leg and instinctively squeezed. A haze descended over my body, and I became a spectator of the exchange—disassociated.

A free high.

She directed me to an alley behind the shopping center. I parked next to some trash bins and shut off the car.

She pulled up her skirt.

Right foot on the dashboard.

Dirty white tennis shoes, and a small tattoo of a heart on her ankle—Jason.

"What do you want?" she said.

I heard myself tell her that I just wanted to jerk off—thinking in some way that I wasn't unfaithful if I didn't enter her. I took my pants off and she slid the seat back. I crawled over and knelt before her.

I'm a big man, and the positioning was uncomfortable, but the struggle did nothing to disrupt the scene.

Her breath was new—the sour taste of failure and dissatisfaction absent.

The gold ring on my finger was taking skin, rubbing me raw, but I powered through—quick, unbridled, left-hand.

Her lips slightly parted, the tip of her tongue gliding across her teeth.

Beautiful…

Unattached…

Less than human…

I was quick.

The guilt was quicker—rising as my cock descended, choking me as I came.

I paid her without looking, dropped her at the corner, and drove home.

I'd promised to make dinner.

The Stray

The old man was awakened by its cries—an animal outside; its wounded voice carrying louder than the trains crossing the overpass below his house.

They were awful—these beasts—unkempt feral animals whose outdoor existence was only encouraged by the soft-hearted do-gooders that brought them food.

If you love them so much, he thought, *why don't you take them in, let them defecate and breed in your neighborhood. But oh no, they're fine out there, they say. They're not hurting anyone. They have rights— just like you do.*

He rose from his bed and pulled on his work boots. He grabbed a flashlight from the kitchen, put a jacket on over his nightshirt, and walked outside.

The animal was wailing tenor-pitched, mournful calls, begging for help.

Ughhh, why can't this fucking thing die?

These beasts were always getting hurt—hit by cars, wandering onto the train tracks, even being abused by some of the older children who lived nearby—not that he was for that. He wasn't cruel. But sometimes after months and years of putting up with all manner of foulness, you just don't give a fuck anymore. You begin to tolerate—if not be gladdened by—the harm being inflicted upon them.

All he wanted was a bit of peace in the evenings.

He'd called the various city and county agencies that dealt with this sort of thing, but their reaction was always the same—buck-passing indifference—placating statements, promising to send someone out. But as of yet…nothing.

He scanned the yard with his light. The cries were coming from out back—behind his fence, the alley that ran adjacent to his place.

He opened the gate with a bit more force than necessary—hoping the noise would drive the beast off, but if anything, the sound only amplified its cries.

He pointed his light in the direction of the wails.

The stray was lying near the trash cans. It was moving—slow motion writhing in the dirt. He walked toward it. There was a trail of blood.

It didn't get hurt here. Maybe it was trying to make its way back to the bushes.

He kicked at its legs with his boot.

What the fuck am I supposed to do, go back to bed and hope it dies within the hour? Nobody's gonna come out here and shut this thing up. Fucking, lower-animal trash—that's all it is. And those Goddamn crusaders… when are they gonna learn not all life is sacred?"

He shook his head and walked back into his yard.

There was a small tarp covering his workbench, he picked it up.

Be a shame to get blood on it, but I don't think I can kill that thing without it being covered.

When he was a young boy, he'd watched his father put down animals on their farm. Nasty business, but his old man was real frontier—kill it and eat it. They don't make 'em like that today.

He wondered if he'd have the stomach for it.

The thought made him retch, but if he didn't kill it, he wouldn't sleep.

He returned to the beast.

The injured animal turned its great head toward him—the light shone painful in what was left of its eyes. The beam touched glowing blue spots on yellowed whites.

It looked as if it might be blind—or maybe cataracts.

His Jim had something like that in his eyes. Twelve years that hound served him—loved him like a child. He had the dignity and the strength to die quietly. Not like this thing.

Jesus, sometimes it looks like they've got a soul—the way they look at you.

"Please," the beast said—he reached out for the man—"help me."

He covered it with the tarp and then stomped on its head until it ceased to cry.

Public Number

I keep a public number; 714-794-5625. I was told long ago—by a man who was desired by no one, that I should make it easy for people to contact me. I have, and they have.

I receive death threats, drunk dials, propositions for free drugs or sex, long rambling messages about someone doing something to someone who shouldn't be accepting it, and often, I get people calling who feel the need to correct or enlighten me.

The other day I got a call from a therapist. This is not her real name.

"Jack, this is Dorothy Ann, could you please call me back?"

She left her number—I won't print it here.

I blocked my digits and used my cellphone to return the call. I usually call back, but I often force people to accept the reality of having to wait for something—meaning, my return call is not often timely. Unless I believe it's a legitimate psychic emergency—and those are few and far between.

Dorothy answered the phone.

"Hi, this is Jack Grisham; I'm returning your call."

There was a pause—a hesitant I-can't-believe-you-called-back-moment and then she spoke.

"Wonderful. I hope you don't find me rude, but I read your work and I was wondering if you might like to come in and talk to me—no charge, of course."

"I'm sorry," I said, "are you offering me a session? Did I offend you in some way?"

"Oh no. It's nothing like that, it's just that—like I said—I read your work, and I'm offering to help."

"Are you an editor? I know I get a little sloppy with the commas sometimes—somebody once asked me if I'm just randomly placing 'em, but I think I'm doing all right."

"No, sweetheart. I'm a therapist. I'm not calling about your grammatical health."

"I don't get it. Do you think I'm ill?"

"Jack, your last story was about killing a homeless man. The one before that, picking up a prostitute. You've written of violence, rage, cross-dressing, sexual acting out, depression, suicide, and—excuse me if I'm mistaken—but I think you even wrote a story about a mother who kills her newborn because she loves him and realizes he doesn't want to be in this world."

She took a deep inhale.

"Would you like to come in for a visit?"

I wish she could've seen me smile.

"Dorothy, I write about disconnection, and my goal is to get my reader to see where others might be hurting. It worked—you called.

I've never been better. I'm in a wonderful relationship, I have a beautiful family, I try to be of service to others, and I live in a space of gratitude and contentment. I don't need your help, but I'd love your friendship."

Another hesitant pause lay between us. I waited for her to speak.

"Wow," she said. "I didn't expect that. As a matter of fact, I didn't expect you to call back. Your offer of friendship sounds wonderful, and if there's ever anything I could do for you, will you please let me know?"

"Thanks Dorothy, there is something you could do for me."

"Anything."

"I have a friend who is thinking about killing his neighbor, and it's gotten to the point that he's masturbating to the thought of it. Do you think you could you give him a call?"

Master Heal Thyself

The Master reached into his pocket, pulled out his last two dollars, and then he dropped them into the man's cup.

"What'd you do that for? They're all on drugs and—fuck, do you know how much money those dudes make a day? Shit, he probably pulls in more than I do."

"I'm not doing it for him, and I don't care what he does with the money—it's not mine."

"What'd you mean, it's not yours?"

"It's not mine. I gave it to him. It's his. He can do what he likes with it."

They walked in silence. The student lit a cigarette and pondered the interaction.

"You seem troubled," the Master said. "What's bothering you?"

"It's just that I'm supposed to be learning from you—and if I can be honest," he paused as if a reply was coming—it wasn't. "I'm not seeing much—an empty wallet and a beater car with what, 300,000 miles on it?""

"Two seventy-six."

"Yeah, and the windshield—how long has that been broken?"

The windshield had been broken for at least a month or two, maybe three—the Master was downtown, ministering to the homeless, and his car had been vandalized.

"I'll replace it when I have a chance. But let me ask you—since you've stepped onto this road, what do you think *you're* worth? If you liquidated today, what are you looking at?"

"You mean the houses, the cars, everything?"

"Yes. It seems as if you're searching for a comparison, so if you could sell it all today, how much are you worth?"

"I don't know, but I guess if I added it up, about three-point-five or four million. Why?"

The Master was silent for a moment, then asked for a cigarette.

"You don't smoke—but okay, I'll play along."

The student handed him a cigarette. The Master held it in his fingers, rolled it back and forth a moment, then crushed it—scattered the tobacco, and put the filter in his pocket.

"What are you doing?" the student asked. "You wasted that smoke."

"Whose was it?" replied the Master.

"It was mine. I mean, it was yours—I guess."

"That's right. It was mine. But you gave it with strings attached—you gave it with the intention that I should do with it as you wished, in the manner you saw fit.

"You came to me because you were unhappy. Your children despise you. Your wife—a woman you found worthy of marriage due to the size of her mammary glands and her ability to swing naked around a pole—is cheating on you. Your company is sliding into the gutter. And you're questioning me about the condition of my car—a tool that does for me as I need. I'm trying to teach you to be content with nothing—for that's what you have. Nothing. You can't even spare a single cigarette."

The student thought a moment, then his open hand became a fist. He threw a hard right cross that lay the Master to the ground—and stormed away.

The Master slowly raised his head and through bleeding lips he called toward the man.

"I'm sorry I woke you," he said. "Go back to sleep."

Don't Baby Me

I could hear their breath—their bedsheets rustling, infant sails unfurled in sterile hospital air. I lay beside them—vulnerable on my bed, my hands clenched, my eyes swollen shut, unaccustomed to the light.

The door opened, and the noise agitated those who lay around me. They screamed and would not be still. I had not the words to reprimand nor comfort them. I was as much a newcomer as they were, but I fought to remain as I was—if not, less than I am now.

Struggling, I became caught in their need, and then I too wailed as they did.

Hard staccato steps proclaimed her approach. My heart echoed in kind. It was me she sought.

I could smell her as she leaned over the crib—her absence of perfume and the scent of another man swam upon her clothes. He smoked, and the acrid smell of his sweat carried the scent of one who labors for his pay.

I did nothing to accommodate her touch.

I would not be hers—never was, never will be.

A heavy male presence entered the room. The others grew silent.

"Have you been able to make contact with him?" he asked.

"No," she said.

The male touched my cheek. His hands smelled of iodine and traces of alcohol—non-medicinal. He used his thumb and fore-finger to open my right eye. A light—he intruded upon it.

"The nurse said he'd opened his eyes, but she also said he refused to look at her."

"Is he healthy?"

"His eyes, yes—he can see, but this non-communication is something that goes much deeper—almost defiance against life."

She gently removed my blanket, and instinctively I sought the warmth of my own body.

"See how he withdraws," the man said. "He can hear, and he can see—but he's refusing food."

The woman placed her hand on my forehead. She leaned towards me, and a tear fell from her eye and landed on my lips—the taste of disheartened salt water filled my mouth. It sickened me.

"Is there anything you can do?" she said.

"We're planning on force-feeding him, but it will only go so far. If he refuses to live, there's not much we can do for him."

I felt his presence exit the room—the door opening and closing, the footsteps fading purposely away.

I felt her breath against my face—her voice whisper-close.

"Your mother loves you, baby, but I'm going to let you go now. I'm sorry for bringing you into a world that you didn't want to live in."

She took the small blanket that I was wrapped in, and held it over my face.

I inhaled the cloth.

She could have other children.

An Anchor Released

On the Northern coast, the light is soft and diffused—there are mists in the air—ghosts, even on the brightest of days.

The door to our house was wide, and an ocean breeze was playing on our stairs. I was sitting in my favorite chair—a large red leather recliner that gave me a clear view of the street.

There was a man standing on the far corner. His head moved like that of a seabird—shifting in quick, darting stabs from house to house—searching.

I stood to walk outside, offer my assistance, but as I rose, he turned and looked directly into my eyes.

He came toward me.

I wasn't afraid, but his presence made me uneasy—my thoughts staggered as they sought solid ground. He looked familiar, but if so, his face had been abandoned, and it wasn't until he reached the threshold of my door that I could put a name to him.

"Michael"—I smiled and offered my hand, which was silently taken in his—a hand not warmed by that winter sun. "Where've you been? I heard you were dead."

"I wasn't sure if this was your house," he said. "I thought it was, but you've changed—you're not what I expected."

"Yeah," I laughed, "I've gotten old."

I asked him inside, and as he entered, he touched the small cross etched into my door.

"Is this you now?" he asked.

"Well, I do prefer forgiveness these days. The hate I discarded years ago."

"Good for me,"" he said. "That's why I'm here. I wronged you, and I speak for your forgiveness."

I knew the crime he spoke of, and the uneasiness of before returned. He'd abused me when I was a child—forcing his way upon me. I let my eyes travel over his face—he hadn't changed, and the shirt and jacket that he wore were familiar.

"Fuck, don't worry about it," I said. "It was a long time ago. I'm over it, and I've done more than my share of hurting people."

"Yes, that's how it goes," he replied. "An anchor thrown into the ocean on a calm day will send waves from ship to shore—miles they travel. And a hurt done to an innocent boy, will also create waves, and miles *they* will travel—although, with boys, the waves can at times become malicious and turn upon themselves."

I thought to my life—the pain I'd inflicted on others, and the harm I had done to myself. It had been years since I'd poisoned my body, and years since that first sober breath, that I'd sought to repair the damage that I'd done. I don't think I'll ever be free of the guilt, but I sleep easier these days—other than the few ghosts that still darken my door.

I had nothing to say. I was ready for him to leave, and as if he read my mind, he walked toward the door, pausing once again at the threshold.

"I hurt you," he said. "I hurt others too—just as the man who hurt me did. I came here because the wave stopped at your feet. I can travel no further from you. You forgave my trespasses as you have forgiven your own. I won't return."

As he turned to leave, a mist wrapped around his body and stole him away.

Desire

She was all he ever wanted. And I don't say that as some trite literary cliché or for bold dramatic flair—it was true. He'd lived his life with a desire for nothing. That's not to say he needed neither air nor food, or that he was beyond the want of basic human necessities. But if he was deprived of those things—if he were somehow placed without—I believe he'd have calmly done so until death.

And so, as one who watches from the fringes of his existence, I was surprised when I saw his heart change—when he developed drive and desire, when he decided that without her, his life was meaningless.

She was a coffee girl. A punkish, grounds-under-the-fingernails slow-bob who struggled while making lattes. If you ordered a muffin or a breakfast sandwich with your drink, you could count on it being improperly heated or replaced with something so unlike what you'd ordered, the mix-up itself felt like a premeditated "fuck you."

She was an idiot. And be it muffin or sandwich, cookie or cake, she was destined to screw it up.

He found her ineptitude adorable.

"I'd like a large black coffee, please." He really wanted an iced mocha, but he didn't want to press the issue.

"Would you like something else?" she asked. "Maybe something to eat?"

"I'd like you to go out with me."

"To go?"

"No, not to go. I'll drink the coffee here. I'd like you to go out with me—on a date. A movie. Even a quick lunch. I'd ask you to coffee, but I'm sure you're sick of it."

"I like my job," she said. "I'm not sick of it."

He picked up his drink from the counter and smiled—his large black coffee was a medium with cream and two sugars.

"What time are you off?"

She replied with a beautiful, empty-headed smile that lit up his morning.

As he walked out the door, he noticed the shop hours neatly painted on a small wooden sign—6 a.m. to 9 p.m.

Hmmm, he thought, *an evening treat of coffee-shop-pie—delicious.*

He had never forcibly abducted anyone before. As I said, he lacked desire. But this newfound prize was something that had to be claimed.

He drove to the carwash and had his car cleaned. He wanted things to be nice for her when he took her for a ride.

At 8:55 p.m., he was parked in the alley behind the shop. He had no rope, no knife, no gun—he considered those things overkill in what would be an abduction by wit.

By 9:30, she still hadn't left.

He walked to the front of the building where he found her struggling with the door.

"Could you help me?" she asked.

"Of course," he said. "I'd love to."

The New Jesus

He was overweight, unqualified, and a total cunt. But he was my boss, and I needed the work.

"I want ten-thousand words on this new Jesus," he said. "Can you do it?"

You want ten? I'll give you a million, you fat prick

"Sure, boss. I'm your man."

"Perfect." He handed me an address and a time. "Go here, talk to the Rabbi, and write it up. They say he's the second coming of Christ. I say he's full of shit."

The address was straight-up downtown, a shit-hole apartment building housing derelicts and section eights. The Lord Our God was three flights up. I climbed the stairs and knocked on the door.

"Hey, Jesus!" I said. "Open up."

I was let in by a prostitute. I knew her—Reckless Mary. She worked the bars on Oliver Street. I brushed her ass as I walked in. She pushed back against my hand.

"Is that what you're looking for, baby? You come up here for ass?"

She was hot, I'll give her that, but I was short on condoms and pressed for time.

"No thanks, I'm…uh…"

"—Looking for me?"

It was the new Jesus. He was maybe five-foot-two—if he thickened up the sandals—and he was fat. I thought my boss was a pig. This holy roller was an easy 300 pounds. Red hair, freckles, and a pair of ears on him that made him look like a clown.

"You gotta be fucking kidding me," I said.

"Why, because I look like this?" He rubbed his belly. "We made a mistake last time—I was too comely. The message got lost under that dashing romantic figure—slim and handsome—you Christians painted me blond, nailed to the cross."

He farted. A foul odor filled the room.

"Oh no, there won't be any of that good-looking martyr business this time around. I'm the new and improved Jesus."

I took in the vibe of the apartment—the couch I was sitting on was more dog bed than settee. The few chairs—chipped Walmart wood. The carpet was torn, stained, and worn. Mary—the prostitute— standing in the kitchen, rubbing her itchy crotch while she sucked religiously on a glass pipe. She tied the whole thing together.

"Yeah, you look new and improved—a short fat bozo living in squalor with a prostitute and a plan. Lose the belly, and it reads just like the old God."

"Yes, it does," he said. "And I knew you—above all people— would be able to see the truth. You will be my voice in the wilderness, John. You will proclaim my coming."

"Ha! Okay then, here's my proclamation: you're full of shit. And anybody that believes in you, or contributes to your cause, is a fucking moron who deserves to be fleeced. I'm gonna recommend the paper doesn't waste print on you."

"Perfect! That's the sort of convicted disbelief I was hoping for. Turning you into a believer will pave the road to heaven with the skins of converts. Could you, uh, call your opinion in—would that "fat prick," as you called him, take your ten thousand words on how I'm a charlatan over the phone?"

"What are you talking about? I didn't call him that."

"Sure, you did." He tapped the side of his head. My voice exited his mouth—*"I'll give you a million, you fat prick."*

Mary cackled in the background as she hit the pipe.

"You humans need proof, and even then, you argue about what you thought you saw—or heard. I'm gonna use you. I'm gonna turn you out."

I was dazed. I would assume that I'd been slipped a mickey, but I'd touched no food or drink since my arrival—Mary's laugh was debilitating as it swirled around me.

"Is she bothering you?" he said. "Easy as done."

He made a grand sweep of his hand. Mary dropped to her knees; the pipe fell from her mouth; she was choking, unable to breathe. Her jaundiced skin faded to a pale olive green. She reached for Jesus.

"What do you say, John? Should I save her?"

Mary became still—a lifeless sinner on a threadbare carpet.

"Do something, man—help her!"

"Why me, John? Why not you?"

"Because I can't, and you can. You told me you were Jesus."

"That's right, my friend. But I'm the new and improved Jesus. I don't waste my magic on gutter whores. Now let's make that phone call."

Bang One Out

"You ever see her before?"

"Yeah, last week; she was here for play-offs."

"Do you know her?"

"No, but Jodie does. I think she used to fuck Marvin."

"Oh, are you shitting me, man? He said she was crazy."

"Nah, not this chick. I think it was the other one; but that's coming from him—he's a fucking idiot."

"Yeah, but he can pull bitches, man—fuckin' A. I'm gonna hit her up."

She had dark, red hair straight out of a bottle—*nobody is that red with that tan.* She was tall, freckles running wild on her face, and ass for days. He'd never been much of an ass man but, Jesus, how could you not be, when you got something like that bouncing around in front of you.

He walked up to the bar and threw her a smile.

He wasn't a douche. He was cool—a man's man. He had no problem catching pussy.

"My buddy says you were here with Jodie. Are you guys friends? Is she coming tonight?"

The redhead looked him over. He was good-looking and tall—stylishly dressed, fit. He could be her type…if he had what it took.

"Yeah. I know Jodie, but tonight I came alone."

She held out a hand that was smooth and strong. "I'm Erin." She had a grip worthy of a steelworker. He dug it.

"Nice handshake, the name's Trent. I used to work with Jodie."

"Trent," she repeated, digesting his vibe. "You look like fun, but they all look like fun in the beginning, don't they?"

"Yeah, I guess so."

"Do you?" she said.

"Do I what?"

"Do you *guess so*—take all your future girls on a hunch? Is that why you're single? I'm assuming you are."

"I wouldn't be talking to you if I wasn't."

"All right, then. You're honorable, and I'm prudent. I don't jump into a relationship on a hunch. I like to know what I'm getting into before I make a move. You come up to me, you look all right, but I want to know if you got what it takes—if you're packing the punch I need to get by. Do you wanna go outside and *bang one out*?"

Trent spit up his beer. "You're crazy."

"No, I'm not. I ain't easy either. Are you a big boy, Trent, or are you just looking to add me to a string of failed romances—bad guesses. I figure we could waste a bunch of time waiting for the wheels to fall off or we could be *getting it on*." She ran her hands down her hips. "Do you want it, or do you want to go back to your buddy and jerk off?"

"Yeah, I uh…"

She stood, downed her drink, and pulled him by the hand.

She led him out the backdoor to the parking lot, leaned against a car, and spread her legs.

"You ready, tough guy?" she cooed.

"Fuck, yeah, I'm ready."

She kicked him in the balls.

He doubled over. She followed with a vicious uppercut to the chin. He turned in time to save his teeth—the intended blow glanced his ear.

He retaliated with an open hand slap that caught her brutally above the left eye. She backed off and squared up.

"How 'bout those balls, bitch?" she hissed.

He was hurting—bad, but he wasn't going to give her the pleasure of knowing he'd be pissing blood.

She moved closer and grabbed his hair with both hands. He spit in her mouth.

They slow danced across the pavement.

"Yeah, baby," she said. "Show me what you got."

He punched her in the tit.

She broke his nose.

He gouged her left eye with his thumb. "Hope you ain't driving, tramp."

He worked her body—hard gut shots that softened her up.

She swept his leg, taking him to the ground.

He climbed on top. It was close combat now—hair pulling, biting, spitting.

Trent felt himself about to cum.

She was closer.

"Yeah, baby," she screamed. "I'm right there, I'm—oh…oh… I'm cumming, baby! I'm cumming!"

As she came, Trent shot in his pants.

It was over.

Spent, they sat near each other on the pavement—they felt good about the exchange.

"I like you," she said, "I think we can do this."

"Sure, baby."

He wiped his bloody nose with his sleeve.

"Why not?"

A Turn on 12th

Brooke and I normally walk down Walnut—we never would've seen her if we hadn't switched it up. But today we turned on 12ᵗʰ, and there she was—across the street, coming out of a cheap apartment near the old Greek diner—looking haggard, carrying her shoes.

"Ouch. Walk of shame, huh? She's wearing last night's clothes."

"Really, babe? Like you've never done it?"

"Sure, I have. I still have a curb mark on my forehead from the last time I went out."

I quick-checked her brow—she wasn't lying.

"Fuck, I know that chick. She used to go to this meeting in the Harbor—real gnarly drunk. I had a coffee with once—chatted a couple times on the phone."

She spotted us—well, me specifically—and the expression on her face morphed from oh-my-aching-head to oh-my-God-there's-that-fucking-sober-guy-and-I-reek-of-booze.

I waved.

She waved back.

I whispered to Brook, "If she comes over, introduce yourself. I can't remember her fucking name."

"I'm sure she's not gonna—" The girl stepped into the street.

Brooke giggled. "Drunken slut at three o'clock."

She crossed over. Brooke stuck out her hand.

"Don't bother," the girl said. "You're only doing that because he can't remember my name. It's Lori, Jack."

"Come on—I remembered. Fucking, Lori."

"Great. Now we're both liars. And it's just, Lori, no fucking."

I was hoping it'd be a quick hi-bye situation, but she just stood there, so I had to speak.

"So, uh...what's up?"

She held up her shoes like they explained her recent transgression.

"You got new shoes. Looking tight."

"Fuck you, Jack. I just woke up on a blow-up bed with some Persian dude breathing stale kebab up my nose. I remember leaving Crabby's, but I'm not sure how I got here. I was hammered—I'm still kinda buzzed. I woke up naked, and my coochie feels like he got a piece. I didn't see any condoms. I picked up the trail of my clothes, got dressed as quiet as I could, and crept out—fuck, there he is."

The "Persian dude" waved from the doorway. He crossed the street.

She leaned on me. "Come on, Jack, help me out here. Don't let this dude—hey, guy!" She forced a smile.

He took us in with his eyes, decided we weren't a threat, and held out his hand.

"Hey, player. I'm Michael."

116

"Michael?" I shook his hand, bro-style. "She said you were Persian."

"Persian? I'm not fucking Persian. My dad's Hawaiian and my mom's from Greece."

"Ah, the mystery of the kebab."

"Where you going, Tori? Can I drive you home?"

She pleaded with her eyes, but it was her mess—her karma to straighten out.

We said our goodbyes, and I helped out the bro: "It was nice to see you, *Lori*, you too Michael.

"You still got my number?"

"Unless you changed it," she said.

"Nope, still good. Call me when you get home. We gotta chat."

We took 12th to the beach.

"Fuck," Brooke groaned. "I gotta get to work. Can we head back?"

"Yeah… I was just thinking—"

"If she was gonna call? She is cute."

"Fuck off, Brooke. That's the last thing I need. I was just wondering…what it's like to see somebody like me—a sober cat—when you're pulling shit like that. That's gotta be fucked."

When I got to my apartment, Lori was waiting on the steps.

"What the fuck? I thought he took you home."

"No fucking way. First off, I don't want that dude knowing where I live. Second, I'm staying with my mom. I'm not bringing some fucking Persian dude over there. She'd shit."

"He's Hawaiian."

"Fuck you. Where's your place."

"Number seven. Second floor."

She climbed the stairs. I paused before following.

"You seeing Brooke?" she asked. "She seemed all right."

"No. We're just friends."

"I didn't want her getting weird about me coming over."

My key was above the door. I hoped it was unlocked (it was)—I didn't want her to see where I stashed it. I let us in.

"This is a great place." She dropped her shoes and walked to the window. "I remember when you moved in here."

"No, you don't. How'd you even know where I live?"

"You were fucking Janet—I'm friends with her." She passed me into the bathroom, patting my ass. "She said you were fun. Do you mind?" She turned on the bath water.

"What the fuck are you doing?"

"Come on, don't be a dick. I stink."

She stripped without shutting the door, walked into the kitchen naked, and poured a glass of water. She had a big bruise on her back.

I kept my mouth shut.

"Come talk to me while I soak."

I brought in a small chair. Watching her bathe wasn't unpleasant.

"You ever try to forget things?" she asked. "I was trying to forget last night when I saw you. I felt so fucking low. I know what you had to be thinking: *this chick is a drunken slut.*"

"I didn't think that. I don't judge you."

"Everybody does. I judged you when you cheated on Janet."

"Come on. That's fucked. What's wrong with you—"

"Don't trip. She deserved it. She was sleeping with Carlos."

For the record, I never thought she was faithful—none of them are.

"If you knew she was fucking him, why was I the bad guy?"

"Because *you* didn't know. You did what you did thinking she was playing straight. You were cheating. It didn't matter what she was doing. You were being deceitful."

She stood. "Get me a towel."

I held it for her. I liked her. I wished she wasn't so fucked up.

The phone rang.

It was Brooke.

"I can't quit thinking about that girl—but for the grace of God go I, right?"

I was glad I hadn't put it on speaker.

Lori touched my arm. "Hey, you got a robe I can wear?"

I nodded toward my closet.

"Who is that?" Brook asked. *"Is someone over?"*

I tried to be discreet. "You can use the blue one, Lori."

"She's there?"

"Uh-huh?"

"Did you fuck her?"

"Come on—Jesus. I gotta go." I hung up.

Lori lay on my bed.

"Was that Brooke?"

"How'd you know?"

"Because you said my name. I'm a drunk, not stupid."

"I didn't think you were."

She piled up pillows behind her. One leg—bare, bruised, and smooth—slid free of the robe. Kissable. Caressable.

"Are you still a hypnotist?"

"Yeah. Why?"

"Can you make me forget what I've done? That's why I came here. If I could forget this shit, I might take better care of myself—quit drinking—stop fucking randoms."

"Sure. I can do it. But it's not right. You're not supposed to block that shit. Your supposed to face it—be so sickened by your own actions that something inside snaps and you wake up. Head down a new path. Reborn in the spirit kind of thing."

"Is that what happened to you? You were reborn?"

"Yeah, I guess so."

"But you still cheated on Janet."

"I didn't say I liked myself."

She closed her eyes for a moment.

"So you picked alcohol and drugs. That was your choice?"

"What do you mean?"

"Out of all your vices, you picked alcohol and drugs. You haven't had a drink in what—thirty-something years?"

"Yeah. Thirty-four."

"But you could've picked lying, or cheating, or your addiction to women—and you didn't. You could've made any of those things the focus, been thirty-four years clean from that, and still acted out on all the rest, including drinking—but you didn't."

"It doesn't work that way."

"Why not? Why the fuck can you stop that and not this? You know I'm a drunk, and I just got fucked raw by a stranger, but you can't stop looking at me. If I wanted, I could have you."

She was right. It was hell to not touch her. I didn't have an answer.

"I want you to black me out," she said. "I've looked deep inside, and even though I'm sickened by what I've done, it hasn't been enough to make me change. Will you do it—remove my memories?"

"Yeah I'll do it. Lie back on the bed and close your eyes."

A Walk in the Park

The great park was as beautiful as he'd ever seen it. For the last twenty years, he'd lived within a window's view of its majesty. He donned his coat and walked across the street. The leaves had turned but had not yet fallen, so above his head a canopy of browns, yellows, reds, and faded greens danced in the treetops. He walked without purpose toward the lake.

"May I have your autograph, Mr. Johns?"

A child looked up at him, her face golden-lit by fall's diffused sunlight. She was an angel—a postcard perfect vision of what eager youth should be. He smiled as he took the pen and notebook she offered. Her mother stood behind, radiating protective encouragement.

"Yes, my dear," he said, as he inscribed his name. "And for your mother—what would she like?"

The woman blushed as she stepped forward.

"I'm sorry Mr. Johns. We don't mean to disturb you, but I... I mean we, we love your work. I was so excited to see you."

He opened his arms. She stepped in, and he pulled her close. She smelled of lavender, coffee, and time spent with loved ones.

"It's good to be seen," he said as he let her go. "Thank you."

As he walked away, the memory of their voices lingered—like nightingales falling through leaves. He had never felt more at peace. And as he strolled the park, the scene replayed again and again— fathers and sons, husbands and wives, lovers. So many lives he had touched. He accepted their praise graciously—albeit a touch awkwardly.

It hadn't always been like this. He was once met with anger and disdain—a reflection of the hatred he'd preached in his early work. But over time, his view of the world changed. His hate gave way to into acceptance, his acceptance to love, and that love became the world around him—and that world, in turn, loved him.

A young man approached—slim, a cloud wavering beneath the trees. Winter grey eyes. Lips trembling with the frost of disillusion.

"Are you Lane Johns?"

Lane reached toward him.

The young man reached back—with lightning flash from his hip.

Lane dropped.

He sat in the path, legs splayed, heaving like a winded child.

The young man stepped closer.

Another flash lit the air. Then another. Lane's coat lifted and tore in the breeze.

Twice more the young man's fury surged, and then he turned, dropped a book in the dirt, and walked away.

Lane struggled for breath.

Screams scattered like gusts of wind across the field.

The world receded. A crowd of hopeless onlookers gathered around him.

By his feet, abandoned by his assailant, lay a copy of his first work. Its title—now partly obscured by blood—read: *Please Kill Me.*

The Incarnation of Ralph

His name was Ralph, and he was locked out again.

Are you fucking kidding me? This shit is getting real tired.

He could see them inside. A warm glow from the fireplace lit their faces on the couch. He scratched at the sliding glass door—voiced his disapproval to the stars—then shot a short wee stream into a pair of shoes left outside.

Bunch of spoiled brats. 'Give me a doggie, Mommy—please, can I, can I?'

He jumped on the backyard table and sent it crashing to the ground.

That'll do it.

The porchlight flashed on. The father poked his head out the door.

"God damn it, Linda. That fucking dog just trashed my succulents."

Ralph jumped over a broken ceramic pot and ran for the warmth of the house. The father threw a kick in his direction.

Good effort, pops. He took no offense at the intended assault. *A man after my own heart.*

"They're just plants, Jimmy. There's no need to get so bent out of shape." She wiped her wet hands on a dish towel. "I bought him, I'll clean it up."

You got that right, bitch. You will clean it up.

She was the perfect codependent. Ralph loved it when she shared the blame—and she was cute too—a lot cuter than that bitch he'd married.

I wonder where she is now? Hooked up with some fucking shaman probably—the two of them eating each other's asses in some patchouli-soaked yurt. Fuck her. It's her fault I'm like this.

I need to seek, Dear—that's what she said—I need to be free to go on a spiritual quest, and I want you to come with me, but if not, I understand; I'll go it alone. Fucking blackmail, bullshit—but what do I do? I fucking go. Love will do that to you. I followed that bitch through Jesus, Buddha, Mohamed—we did it all. Then I go and die right in the middle of that Hindu crap, and here I am—reincarnated as a fucking dog. A bullshit, sissy-assed, labradoodle—motherfuck.

"Ralph!" She called from the bedroom.

He scurried in, jumped up on the bed, rolled over, and spread his legs. She started scratching.

"That's a good boy," she said. "They shouldn't have left my baby outside."

You goddamn right, they shouldn't have. I'm the swinging dick in this hovel.

128

Ralph wiggled on his back. He loved this shit. He slid toward her, hoping her hand would drop to his balls.

That's it, darlin'. Grab that shit and start tugging.

His pointy pink cock popped out from its hairy sheath.

"Ughhh." She pushed him to the floor. "God damn it, Ralph."

He hunched down on all fours and dragged his ass under the bed.

Really? You buy me, bring me home, keep me chained up like a slave, and then you don't give me the courtesy of a hand-job?

He finished himself off with his tongue.

After he came, Ralph wandered into the kitchen and licked his food bowl clean.

I guess it's not so bad. I could've come back as a thousand other beings—I bet a rat could be a real drag. At least these fuckers like me.

The mother bent down and stroked his back. The father smiled pleasantly upon him.

"Linda," he said, "I'd think he'd be better behaved if we had him fixed."

The Police Truck

Some people might call it kidnapping—his idea of offering free rides—but to Robert A. Jones, he was doing a service: helping the boys in blue and ridding the city of unwanted trash.

"Did you know, darling, the vagrancy rate is going up?"

His wife ignored him—or rather, she chose to live together in silent contemplation.

"I think we might need to step up our game. Even up the odds so to speak."

Robert and his wife lived near the park in what was once considered a safe little area—a place where your child could play outside without needing a sentry tower.

"Oh, we had our problems," he'd say to anyone who'd listen, "but there was a sense of family—of honor, of trust—before these unwelcome travelers came in and tore apart the moral fabric of our town."

Robert was a man of action. At 67, he'd learned to use the Google icon on his search bar.

Hmm, how to remove vagrants and undesirables?

He typed *police truck*. Seven hundred and thirty-five million results appeared—along with Robert's hope that the moral fabric would soon be stitched.

"Look here, dear," he said. "I'm not the only one who wants to clean up the streets. There's even a song."

He clicked the link.

"Here you go, Poopsie. Give it a listen."

It was a tune by the band *The Dead Kennedys*. He didn't like their name and thought the guitar was too *Jan and Dean*, but the lyrics were wonderful.

"*And ride, ride, how we ride*," Robert croaked along in his sixty-seven-year-old baritone voice. "I think today I'll buy a vehicle. Tomorrow night, I'll ride."

Back to the search bar.

And as luck would have it, a nineteen-seven-and-seven drunk buggy was for sale in his area. Chrysler-built—before the company went tits up—and in excellent condition, according to the seller.

Robert called his friend, William, an octogenarian he'd met at the Senior Center. William ran hot. Retired military. Still ready to serve.

"Can we wear uniforms?" William asked.

"You can wear whatever you want, buddy. The trash we'll be picking up won't notice anyway. And yeah, uniforms sound fun."

The two men drove to the address. The truck was everything they hoped for.

Robert climbed into the rear compartment.

He closed his eyes and caught the faint scent of dried urine, wine, and fear still residing—within its cool metal walls.

"Are you gentlemen ex-police?" the seller asked.

Robert smiled—his dentures shifting just a touch. "I'm not sure if you're ever not a policeman." he said. "I like my community clean and tight as does my partner. Right, Will?"

William was already in the driver's seat.

"Yes, indeed, Robert. Will we be getting billy clubs, or do we need guns?"

The seller gave Will a look. Robert, ever the community diplomat, deflected.

"Jesus, Will. One day your kidding is gonna get you thrown in the hoosgow. Better stick to your cane."

They all laughed. The deal was sealed. The truck was theirs.

"You look good in black," Robert said, admiring Will's uniform.

Four hundred dollars in government allotment had bought them two full getups: black tactical outfits, boots, handcuffs, two large Maglites, and a case of extra-strength pepper spray—senior discount.

"I think we should've gone with blue," William said. "Y'know, *the boys in blue.*"

"Nah, blue's for your everyday cop. Beat-walkers and traffic stoppers. We're special forces—task force midnight."

"I can't be up that late."

"Check it out, Will! Right there—a good one."

A transient lay beside a dumpster. A few spent bottles of suds lounged by his feet.

It was only 6 p.m. A promising night.

Robert pulled the truck beside the man—blocking view from the street.

As he stepped out, he heard a loud, *fisst*, like spray paint—and the unmistakable *thunk* of a stick hitting skull. Multiple times.

Will had already moved in. Pepper-sprayed and clocked the transient.

"I got this one, Robbie—whoo-eeee!"

"Fuck, Will!" The guy wasn't moving. "You killed him."

"Did not." Will nudged him with a boot. "Least I don't think so. I busted plenty of heads in my day. Ain't swinging as hard as I used to. Hell getting a breath though." He leaned against the truck.

"All right, well help me get him in the back."

Robert opened the doors, grabbed a leg. The man was ripe.

"How are we gonna lift him? I can't do it alone."

Will wheezed. "I guess we should load 'em before we beat 'em. You wanna leave this one?"

"Yeah, maybe. Kinda defeats the purpose though. We're supposed to ship them out, not leave them lying around."

"Well, I'm sure there's a learning curve, Robbie. This was good practice. Next one: load first, beat after." He wiped off his glasses. "Hey, think we should we spray 'em first?"

"Yeah, that seems right. Let's give it a shot."

By 10 p.m.—an hour before Will's bedtime—they'd hit their stride.

She Lives?

"So, you see, Jim, while your wife is dead in this world, she exists in a universe parallel to our own. She still lives."

Jim sat disbelieving upon the sofa. His right hand nervously stroked his temple, then his cheek—his attempt to hold in the tears.

"But I can't touch her," he said. "I can't hold her—smell the scent of cigarettes in her hair. You know, she'd tell me she hadn't been smoking, tried to hide it from me, but then I'd pull her close—tackle her onto the bed—and I could smell that tarnished air trapped in her hairspray. Unmistakable. I knew she was lying."

He managed a weak smile with trembling lip and dropped his effort to be strong.

"I miss her. I've tried to move on, but I can't. I have this feeling that she's still here—in the next room, or coming home late from work. But she's not gone. There has to be a way to reach her."

The doctor lowered the lights in the room.

"Jim, the universe is made of spheres—countless worlds, each creating another, on into infinity. And the soul—or consciousness—

creates matter. Your wife and yourself exist on many different levels, and if you are willing and open to receive her, I think I might be able to help you shift into a parallel world and reunite with your wife. Is that something you'd want to do?"

"Are you kidding? With all my heart."

"Okay then. I want you to lay back, close your eyes, and think of a time where there was conflict in your lives."

"Conflict?" Jim sat up. "Why that? I don't want to think of the bad. I want to think of the good—her kiss—her laughter."

"Jim, listen to me. In times of conflict, there is always an expansion of energy. Have you ever heard of a fork in the road—two or more different pathways emerging from a single event?"

"Of course."

"Well, I'm going to take you back to that event. And instead of following the path you took, you're going to move in another direction. Your consciousness will shift into that alternate world—a world where your wife doesn't take her own life, but seeks help and lives. Now tell me of a time."

A tear escaped a closed eye.

"I feel awful. My behavior is nothing to be proud of.

"Early morning—five or six a.m.—I found a text on her phone. A photo of her and another man. In bed. Kissing.

"I was furious. I became unhinged—beating her until she promised never to see him again.

"She was my wife, and I'd kill for her... or kill her."

"That's it. Hold it. Let it burn. Keep your eyes closed. Listen to my count. Feel yourself tumbling backwards, cartwheeling toward that day—tumbling... turning...there you are. Is she... ?"

"Yes!"

He could smell the scent of her perfume.

The sheets sticking to his back. The weight of her next to him.

He woke and looked into her eyes.

This time he would be silent.

He wouldn't confront her. Wouldn't raise a hand.

She lived.

"I love you," he said. "I love you, my darling."

"I love you too, Jim. But I'm leaving you for Michael."

An Unsatisfactory Meal

"Jack! What's up?"

I barely knew him—certainly not enough to stop and say hello. He was one of those random, hey-man-I-saw-you-back-in-the-day dudes that I often encounter—and just for your sake, if you ever do run into me, and you're thinking of saying hello, please do. I love visiting, and I'm grateful for your attention, but know this—I can barely remember yesterday, let alone an alcohol-hazed evening from thirty-something years ago. And as for shows? Good luck. I've played all over the world—with a thousand different bands—and I've got no idea when or where.

Anyway... I was expecting a quick head nod and a pleasant see-you-around, but he turned and pressed a chat.

"How you doing?" he asked.

"Doing okay. Out for my walk."

I exercise daily—three or four miles of bike path, the pier, and then I wander down Main Street and check the mail. I was ready to get back at it. He was hungry for a story.

"Hey," he said, "you've really been in it, huh? How's it going?"

He was implying that I'd been in a tough spot—I had. A recent separation from my wife, homelessness, and lack of a car had me down on one knee—down, but not out. I'd kept the drama off social media, but it seems this dude had caught the scent of anti-romance. He was fishing—looking for a mid-morning snack.

"Nah," I said, "things are really good, bro—real tight."

He was disappointed. The look on his face was of a seagull who'd dropped a crust of bread.

"Oh, I thought you were homeless or something."

Now, normally I'd leave this dude as is—wish him a nice day and go on about my business—but I hate these fucking drama hunters. You know the type: relishing misfortune because it makes them feel better about their own fruitless existence. I decided to stuff his gut with heartbreak and bullshit tales of bad behavior. I looked out over the ocean, put on a sad face, and then I dished.

"Well, to be honest, bro…"—he leaned close, licking his lips—"I fucked up. I'm on the fucking street, man. I was just walking over to the beach shower to get cleaned up."

"Jeez—I'm sorry to hear that."

No, he wasn't.

"Fucking babysitter, man. These little chicks grow up so fast. I was driving her home—she's seventeen or something—but I guess she didn't have a license or whatever, so my wife asks me to help out. Anyway, I'm giving this little chick a ride—baby girl, sexy as fuck—and she starts flirting with me. Smiling, twirling her hair, playing with her tongue—you know how they do it. You've seen it."

"Yeah, I've seen it—no fucking way, man."

If he was any closer, we'd have been dancing. I could see the beads of sweat forming on his fat, hungry face.

"So, she starts telling me how she digs my band and how stoked she is to help out with the kids—grateful, you know—and then she reaches over and, I shit you not, she puts her sweet little hand right on mine."

"No."

"Yeah. I tried to derail her. I laughed—told her I was older than her father—three times."

"You didn't."

"Fuck if I didn't. She was hot, but I'm not stupid."

The disappointment momentarily returned to his face...until I winked.

"I'm just weak."

"Oh, yeah."

I almost stopped after his '*oh, yeah*'—I mean the fucking bile rose up in my throat watching this lecherous clown digging in. But just for you, I swallowed, and stepped on it.

"I pulled the car over at the park on Gothard—you know the dark lot in the back?"

"Yeah, of course."

I figured he'd been there before.

"Anyway, we pull in, and I'm hoping that maybe if things look like they're going down, she'll get scared and wanna bail—but she doesn't. She takes off her top—tells me to kiss her."

"Did you?"

"Wouldn't you?"

"Yeah, I guess so, but weren't you…"

"Worried about getting caught? Fuck yeah, I was worried. But then she does something I've never seen in my life—and you know I've seen some stuff—but nothing like this. Not ever. And probably never will again. *Unfucking-believable*, man. She leans up and she's got the most perfect little—shit, hang on. I gotta get this."

I lifted my phone to my ear.

"Hello?"

His mouth was hanging open—begging for the dirt that was sure to come.

I was talking to no one.

"Shit—hold tight, dude, it's my ex."

He waited—hungry. And as I began my phantom conversation, I slowly moved away—little by little. Talking and moving, walking and talking, glancing back over my shoulder—waving as he stood there.

Then I turned my back on that motherfucker and boogied off down the street.

I had mail to check, and I wasn't about to satisfy that drama-seeking fuck.

Savage

The clothes were selected by his handlers. It was the costume of a city gentleman—a suit of darkest sable. He turned this way and that; the mirror revealed the sharp pleats to the pants, the razor-blade lines of his lapels. He laughed when he thought of a jaguar clothed in this manner—an alligator wrapped in this cloth—*They say I'm more than these things—more than the greatest beasts on earth.*

The suit hid the scars on his back, the tattoo of his first wife on his chest, and at present, it held in his desire to drink. He was civilized.

There was a line of converts waiting to enter the church, and he took his place at the end of a long tail of sinners. He was a new man, they said—reborn in the Word. He wished the newness would seep from his soul to his back—years of toiling in the bush had crippled him—and yet his mind remained strong. It was as if it had never grown older—his thoughts were immortal.

Looking over the line, he saw a few of his kind—every sixth or seventh soul carried that skittish desperation to bolt the queue and run back to the wilderness. He thought of the tale of the wolf—how they became a servant to man. They were enslaved by comfort—shed the strength of their souls and became dogs. He remembered asking his father why there were still wolves—why they hadn't all changed. His father told him that there was one wolf who wouldn't be swayed, who held true to his nature, and it is his line that you see today. A wolf will chew off his foot to escape the traps of man. A dog will beg for a scrap and a warm bed at his master's feet.

He caught the eyes of one he knew—Inon Sanken—he tended the fields in a village not far from his own. There is much to say in a glance; and whether he caught the reflection of his thoughts in Inon's eyes or whether they thought the same and their mutual shame sparked connection, there was communication there, more so than just acknowledgement.

He made fists of his hands and then he broke his stare.

A group of men exited the church and walked down the line. They were well-fed, well dressed, and well-rehearsed in their words. The heaviest of the set strode toward him.

"Welcome, boys," the man called. "Salvation is before you. Blessed are the meek, for they will inherit the earth."

"Blessed are those who are persecuted because of righteousness," he replied, "for theirs is the kingdom of heaven."

"What's that you say, brother?" the well-dressed pig stopped and laid a fat hand upon his shoulder.

"Reciting my verses, sir; learnt in childhood."

"Good, boy," the man said, and he continued down the line.

"Righteous? What is it to be righteous? Isn't it to be virtuous, justified, and upstanding?"

He looked down the line, singling out those he knew.

"We are these things, to us, not to them. We must be true to ourselves. Is it so righteous to pull men away from the path they chose, to force your version of morality upon those that believe otherwise, to clothe them as you feel a man should wear—to enslave them through comfort. And what of those who go against the purity of soul, who break and crawl their way onto the bosom of your ministry, suckling from your opulence?"

He unbuttoned his coat and let it drop.

His undershirt he pulled over his head and the black line drawing of his first wife blinked in the sun. He kicked off his shoes and removed his pants. He stood naked among the others. His body tanned and weathered. He stepped away from the line and reached toward the stars.

His fingertips scraped the heavens.

His soul inhaled to life—his spirit reborn—the perfection of his existence realized.

"Blessed are the pure in heart," he said, "for they shall be gods."

The Dating Game

Beneath the scent of gasoline and torn vinyl seats hung a residue of sweetness—an innocence that she'd been unable to discard when she butchered her hair. Her once-sunshine blonde strands were now a chopped deep blue-black—Clairol 52d.

She leaned her newly mutated self against me. Her finger—high school smooth—came to rest upon my lips.

"Do you know how much I hate you?" she said.

The headlights from a slow-moving car ran their way across her chest and climbed along her throat. She wore a choke chain collar secured with a small master lock. I nipped at her hand.

"Is that why you hang out with me, so you can replay the emotion?"

"I was looking in the mirror, asshole—but yeah, I hate myself, that's why I hang out with you. You don't give a fuck about me."

That wasn't true. Tonight, was all about her. She had money and a car and a friend of hers was gonna get us on the list. I was acting as a whore—trading cock for an evening out.

"I know you're using me," she said.

"Come on, Becky, I—"

"Don't bother—I get off on it."

She opened her legs, and I crawled between them. I could taste the not-so-subtle notes of Wild Red Berry wine on her breath. Her homework was thrown across the backseat. She had an "A" in History.

She pulled me closer and told me not to cum inside her—too late.

I'd finished as soon as I entered, and now it was hard to continue.

I was bored.

"I could change you," she whispered. "You need someone that understands."

I'd been in therapy since third grade. They understood when I stabbed my sister.

"My mom said you could stay in our garage."

Great. She was fucking her dog.

I kept at it.

When a young man cums, they quickly lose interest—but thankfully, God in his infinite wisdom, gave us teens the ability to get hard again—almost immediately. I was waiting for this to happen, but her talk of changing me was nauseating—off-putting, and not erotic in the least.

I was done.

I pretended to see someone—abruptly rolled off her, and yanked up my pants.

"What are you doing?" she said.

"It's a cop."

"It's not a cop."

"Fuck you, he's standing right there."

She jumped up in the seat and pulled her dress down over her knees—straightened her hair.

"What does he want? He looks angry."

She was taking this further than I'd intended. I was using an imaginary shadow figure to excuse my flaccid state. She was talking about a real-life figure that was standing at my window.

He knocked on the glass with his flashlight.

"This is private property," he said.

In stereo, a knock hit her side of the car—"Why don't you come on out of there?"

I opened my door and exited.

They weren't cops—regular dudes, mid-40s, nothing you could call outstanding—at least, nothing visual. I took a shot on explaining.

"We were just hanging out. We weren't drinking or anything. I'm sorry, man. I guess we parked on the wrong road—took a bad turn."

The man from my side spoke—"Fuck, Ronnie, it's just a couple of kids"—he smiled at me—"We've had a few break-ins."

Becky climbed out of the car.

She was less nervous than I was. I knew I was guilty. She was innocent and still naïve enough to think the law was sacred, and the majority of people were good. Her, I'm-not-in-trouble-I-didn't-do-anything attitude was kinda cute.

"She doesn't look like a kid to me"—Ronnie was a prick.

"I'm 18, asshole."

"She's got the mouth of a big girl too, doesn't she?"

My guy put his hand on my back and pushed me toward the car—"Why don't you two get the fuck out of here and don't come back."

I was happy to oblige, and Becky, tried to follow suit.

Ronnie grabbed the keys from her hand—"Yeah, fuck that, man—a couple of fucking punks looking to vandalize my shit"—he grabbed her by the hair—"Not this time, fucker—get that one!"

My guy came behind me and put his flashlight across my neck—tightened up on it and choked me.

"I'm not fucking resisting, man."

He walked me backwards toward Becky. She'd been thrown to the ground. I was pushed down beside her.

Ronnie took the lead—"Get that fucking rope. I don't want them running off."

"You're not tying me up, asshole"—Becky tried to stand. He stomped her—with no more consideration than a bug on a sidewalk. I went for him, and he lit in on me.

I've been beaten before—my pops has a heavy hand—but fuckin' A, this was quick and hard, and he knocked the shit out of me. I didn't give a fuck about anything—not her or me; I didn't even know what happened.

When my wits returned, I scooted on my rear until my back was against the car. I had my feet and ass on the ground, my knees to my chest—breathing hard. Becky was all right. Her face was red where he kicked her, but she wasn't crying. Maybe she was stunned too.

"You little fuckers want to be punk, do you? You know what that means—punk?"—My guy threw some rope on the ground. He stood back—"Jared knows what a punk is, yeah?"

"Fuck off, Ronnie. If you're gonna do it, just do it."

Ronnie pulled a buck knife from a holster on his hip. He licked the blade with his tongue.

I was wide awake now.

I've been stabbed before. It fucking hurts—bad.

"Come on, man—don't fucking kill us! We weren't doing anything—we're sorry, alright."

"No. It's not alright"—Ronnie kicked at the dirt, rubbed his crotch—he shook me off—"fucking crybaby."

He looked to Jared.

"What do you think, lover boy? You make the call. Here's your chance to get off easy"—he touched Becky's hair—"I don't care who sucks it, you or one of them"—he squeezed his junk—"but this cock is getting sucked."

"Will you let us go then?" Becky said, "If we do it?"

Ronnie knelt down in front of her. "See, fucker—that's what I'm talking about"—he touched her lips—"you gonna take care of me, little girl?"

"No, not me. He'll suck it."

"What the fuck? I'm not gonna do that—" I slid away from her.

"Why not? You told me to park here. You got us into this. Why should I do it?"

"Because I…"

"Because what? Because I'm a girl? Eat shit, asshole—you suck it"—she looked back at Ronnie—"do him, and let us go."

"Ha! That a girl"—Ronnie unzipped his pants—"I like her."

He pulled his jeans off his hips. It was dark, but even in that haze of low light, I could see that his underwear was stained—dirty.

"Come on, man—fuck this! Just let us go, dude," I pled to Jared. "He's just fucking around, right—he ain't gonna do it."

Jared said nothing.

Ronnie's cock was thin, and from where I was on the ground, he looked uncut. He pinched it between his thumb and finger and shook it like a maid getting wrinkles off a sheet.

Becky laughed. "Pencil dick."

"What'd you fucking say?" Ronnie kicked her.

"I said at least you got a pencil dick—he's not gonna be choking on that."

"You fucking bitch—I'll beat your fucking ass. Jared, get the fuck over here!"

Becky was freaking me the fuck out—hey, remember you got an A in history, baby—mommy bought you that car—

Ronnie put his left arm around Jared's shoulder and undid Jared's pants with his right. He reached into his friend's underwear and grabbed Jared's cock—"Here," he said, as he lifted the enormity into the moonlight—"maybe he'll choke on this."

His piece was obscene—a joke—a true-life dildo toy that you'd use to threaten bridesmaids at a bridal shower. It couldn't be real.

"Becky, what the fuck, man—okay dude, come on, you had your fun, now let us go. We're sorry—I swear to God, we'll leave."

Ronnie walked Jared forward—"Take your pick, cocksucker. Who's it gonna be?"

"No one—do her, man. Fuck. Her, not me, guy. She's made for this shit—come on, bro. Let us go. I'm not gonna say a fucking thing."

Ronnie laughed—"You better hope *she* doesn't say a fucking thing."

"Becky come on, Baby, I'll—"

"You'll what—let me, let you, use me again?"

"No, I promise, I'll…"

Ronnie stepped behind me and held my hair. He put the knife against my throat—pulled me to my knees. He stank—piss, sweat, and ass.

Becky giggled—"I wish I had a camera—you're such a fucking tool."

Jared held his cock in front of my mouth—"It's not gonna suck itself, sweetheart."

He force fed me as Ronnie pushed down with the blade—cutting skin. I opened my mouth as wide as I could—trying not to touch it; even so, he complained about my teeth.

I gagged, caught my breath, gagged again. When Jared came, I choked—tried to spit, but Ronnie held my head in place, until his buddy was spent.

Laughing, he pushed me to the ground.

I wiped the inside of my mouth with my sleeve.

Becky sat as if she had nowhere else to go—unfazed.

They left us there on the ground near our car—walked off and into the darkness as if they were out for a calm evening stroll.

I didn't know what I felt.

Becky got behind the wheel and drove us out.

I didn't question her taking me to her house.

I didn't say anything when she walked me to the garage.

She pulled a sleeping bag down from the rafters and laid it out for me. I used a hefty bag of old clothes for a pillow.

"My mom goes to work at 9," she said. "If you have to take a shit in the morning, there's a Wendy's on the corner."

She walked out and I lay there staring at the roof.

Mother's Day

He could hear her breathing in the bedroom—low, alcohol sodden inhales and exhales sending stale air staggering across the bedsheets. Occasionally, a wet Dewar's burp belted from her mouth and rudely traversed its way into the living room.

She was his mommy, and he was hoping she'd be passed-out until morning.

He rose from the sofa and went to find the broom.

There was broken glass in the kitchen.

The beautiful crystal vase of roses that he had given her yesterday had been swept from the counter and onto the floor. He'd cowered when her great arm rose high into the smoke-filled air of the kitchen. Her bicep—larger than his thigh, rippling in the haze; the mounds of soft discolored flesh serving as a cheap-gift assassin for her pleasure.

"Richard!"—she was awake—"Are you out there?"

"Yes, Mommy."

"Mommy wants her baby."

He opened the bedroom door and peeped in.

His mommy was sitting up in bed. She had pulled off her nightie and was drunkenly rubbing her breasts.

"Get your things, baby," she said. "Mommy is feeling naughty."

"Don't you think you should rest Mother?"

She glared at him—cold dagger fury slow boiling over a pale pink bedspread.

"Don't you think you should SHUT THE FUCK UP?"

"I'm sorry, Mommy. I…"

"Who do you think you are, little man? You don't speak to your mother that way. Mommy calls the shots here.

"Now get your goddamn things and report back ASAP."

Richard hustled to the closet and retrieved a large brown suitcase—its edges worn rough; its cheap vinyl handle was two sordid nights away from breaking.

He sat it on the foot of the bed.

"Don't forget your diapies."

"Oh, mom."

"Rickie, Mommy is getting angry. You don't like it when Mommy gets mad."

He took off his shirt, pants, and underwear—folding each piece neatly in turn, and then he removed his socks and rolled them into a ball.

He stood five-foot-six, one-hundred-thirty pounds, and except for his pencil thin mustache, he was hairless as a newborn.

"Come here. Let Mommy see you."

Richard moved toward the head of the bed. His mother held out her arm. Her palm upturned.

"Park it right here."

Richard spread his legs and straddled her hand. He sank down until his meager genitalia were lying upon it.

"Mommy's sorry she broke the vase, Rickie. You're a good boy, aren't you?"

"Yes, Mother. I am good."

She squeezed a bit harder than necessary.

"But you're not that good...are you?"

Richard felt his small cock stiffen—a nervous ripple touched his heart. He hung his head.

"No, Mommy," he said. "I've been bad."

She struggled toward the edge of the bed. Her large body moving across the sheets in waves.

"Help Mommy up."

She rose from the mattress and towered over him—her thick layers of flesh cascading toward the ground.

She tottered to the foot of the bed.

"Open your case, baby—so Mother can see what you have."

As she sifted through his things—whip, paddle, ball-gag, and chain, Richard quailed in anticipation. She wasn't one for routine.

"I'm thinking of something we haven't done in a while," she said. "you've been getting a bit stodgy, haven't you?"

"Yes, Mother."

"It's Mommy, Richard. I'm your mommy"—she settled on a thick pink plastic enema bag and a thin rubber hose—"Ah, just the thing for a constipated little boy. Come with Mommy, Rickie."

He took her hand, and they made their way into the bathroom.

"Here we are—into the tub now, ass up."

He knelt on the cold porcelain interior of the bathtub, his head hanging, eyes closed, his ass prominently displayed.

"Spread your cheeks, Baby. We're going to wash the bad away."

"Yes, Mommy. Thank you. Thank you, Mommy."

A Perfect Cunt

My girlfriend was known for bad decisions—one, falling in love with me; another, letting her good buddy Riff-Raff, practice his tattooing skills on her freckled young hide.

Her left shoulder carried a retarded tiger in pajamas. On her lower stomach, a portrait of Popeye—who, I later found out, was her grandfather. He looked nothing like that salty old sailor.

When she cleaned—discarded the pills, the booze, the occasional line of blow—she decided to get her tattoos removed. Said she wanted a fresh start and a new body to go with her new spiritual self—she threw in a set of double-D titties while she was at it.

One day, she asked me to go to the plastic surgeon.

She doesn't, and I'm grateful—I've got my own shit to do—but that day I was in trouble. Couldn't be trusted home alone.

I got caught screwing the delivery chick at the Thai place, so I was on lock-down. Twenty-four-hour escort.

I was waiting in the lobby when she walks in. Gorgeous—tall, shapely, blonde—wrapped in that California Barbie doll thing I don't usually go for. But she had an exotic edge too—couldn't quite put my finger on it. A slight slant to her eyes maybe. Perfect lips.

In a plastic surgeon's office, you expect fake—doctored, blown-out—but if a doctor built this one, he was a fucking maestro.

I smiled.

She smiled back.

I caught myself daydreaming—taking her out, banging her in the backseat of my girlfriend's car.

I don't know how long I was sitting there, but it got warm, uncomfortable. I took off my sweater. She followed—set down her book and slid off a sweet leather jacket. Underneath: a plain white blouse, short-sleeved.

I checked for a ring—nothing.

Figured I might as well eye-fuck her—didn't look like I was trespassing. My gaze moved from her hand to her wrist, her elbow, then up to the word Cunt—tattooed in a childlike scrawl on her shoulder.

What the fuck?

What kinda idiot would mark up something that looked like her? And that ink wasn't faded—it was black as my soul on white skin. Fresh. That had to be some kinda damage, she uh—

"Can I help you with something?" She caught me staring.

"I'm sorry...I—"

"My arm, right?"

"Yeah. Just surprised to see something like that on you."

"A tattoo?"

"Well... *that* tattoo. Getting it removed?"

"No. I'm in here for this." She lifted her hair.

I imagined my kisses crawling all over that neckline.

"I have a small spot. My hairdresser suggested I get it checked out."

"Yeah, I'm sure that's a good idea—she'd know, right?"

"I guess. I can't see back there. What are you getting looked at?"

"I'm here with my, uh…"—*fuck, this was hard*—"girlfriend. She made some bad tattoo choices. Now she's getting them burned out—I mean off—she's getting them burned off."

We both laughed.

Things were moving along nicely.

"Ellen—oh my God—what are you doing?"

"Tracy?"

"Yes! I can't believe it!"

My girlfriend came bouncing into the waiting room and hijacked our conversation.

"You guys know each other?" I asked as she kissed my cheek.

"We went to school together—Girl Scouts."

She hugged the object of my newfound attraction. The attraction hugged back. They reminded me of long-lost sisters.

"I can't believe it," she said. "Ellen. Where've you been—where'd you go?"

"My mom and dad got divorced and we—"

"Ellen Roberts?" A nurse called from an open door.

My girl was bummed. "You can't go." She grabbed Ellen's arm. "I won't let you!" They laughed and hugged again. "You've gotta come see us."

The nurse called again. "Ellen?"

"I'll come tonight, okay?"

"Yes—of course. I can't believe it."

They exchanged numbers as the nurse led her away.

"Oh my God. I love her!"

I was tired of hearing it. Thirty minutes in the car. An hour in the bedroom. Another hour during sitcoms—she knows I love Choked.

"Aren't you happy for me?"

"Of course, I am, but…"

"You don't understand—we were inseparable. I was devastated when she left."

"Why didn't you guys stay in touch?"

"Because she was just gone. Her mom moved them out. I was only eight—I didn't understand. My mom said Ellen's father was an alcoholic. I could never sleep over. I think he might have hurt her—you know, he shot himself after they left."

"Really?"

"Yeah. I heard my parents talking. My mom said she couldn't believe he blamed it on Ellen."

She sat in quiet thought.

I was glad she found her friend again, but…what about me?

"You wanna get something to eat?"

"Are you kidding? Can't you just call out?"

"Why?"

"Ellen."

"What about her?"

"She's coming over—haven't you been listening?"

"Sweetheart, I love you, but you guys barely talked. How do you know she's gonna—"

She answered her phone—"Ellie!"

And just like that it was on again. Five more minutes of *Oh-my-God-I-fucking-love-yous* before she hung up.

I followed her upstairs.

She ignored me while she cleaned the house. When she made the bed and lit candles and incense in the bedroom, I'd had enough.

"What are you fucking doing—this is ridiculous."

"Please. Don't be an asshole, sweetheart—she was my first kiss."

"What?"

"Yeah, and we slept naked with our arms around each other."

"You were what, eight? I slept naked with a fucking Bugs Bunny doll."

"You don't think she's pretty?"

"Yeah but…"

She wrapped her arms around me—kissed me on the lips. "You don't think it'd be fun?"

Now, if you've been in this situation, you know the shaky ground I'm standing on. Do I think she's crazy? Yeah. She hasn't seen this chick in twenty-something years, and now she thinks they're hopping in bed—me included.

Do I want in? Are you fucking kidding?

The trick is getting in while still giving my girlfriend the right amount of attention. If you're not careful, this kind of deal turns into an emotional nightmare. You gotta be real cool about this shit.

"Tracy—you're out of your fucking mind."

"I am not. Girls can feel this sort of thing."

"You don't even like girls."

"I like her. And we've talked about this before."

"Yeah, while we're fucking—it's called dirty talk."

She kissed me again. "And you're so good at it, baby." She stripped, dropped her clothes in the hamper. "If she gets here before I'm out of the shower, let her in."

I sat on the couch and got my head straight.

Go along with whatever happens. Act disinterested. Try to get Ellen's number. If you get a chance to fuck her, be good. Remember— Tracy comes first. You can fuck her friend later.

A knock hit the door. Right on time.

Jesus, if she was pretty before, she was unreal now.

"Come on in. Tracy's in the shower."

She hugged me. Kissed my cheek.

"I feel like we're family now. I hope you don't mind."

Are you fucking kidding—I support incest in all its dimensions.

We sat on the couch. Same outfit as earlier, minus the jacket. Her blouse was a few buttons south of closed—I could see her bra.

"Did Tracy tell you we were lovers?"

"You were eight—what the fuck is it with you guys?"

"Eight? She's being ridiculous. We were sixteen."

And this, my friends, is what you call a conundrum—you're plexed that your girlfriend's lying—you're wondering what other kind of shit she's been up to, but you don't want to get pissed or put her on the defensive, because your odds of banging this incredibly beautiful woman just shot way up. You can't blow it.

"I guess she was fucking with me"—*be cool now*—"as if I wouldn't support that union."

I smiled.

"Did she tell you about my father?"

Ughhh, how do you handle this—

"I'm not sure what she told me. She said something, but—"

"You don't listen to her?"

"Of course, I listen to her—but she lied about the eight thing and..."

"He killed himself. You asked about my tattoo—he did it. Got drunk—like always, beat me up, marked me. Then blamed me for the marriage."

"You were a teenager—that's fucking awful."

"I guess. My father was an asshole and a liar. He was cheating on my mother. I told her. He was furious."

"I can't imagine. Why don't you get it removed?"

"Never." She came at me hard. "I redo it every year—the day he shot himself." She ran her hand across the mark. "Fifteen years and twenty-six days ago. I'll never forget it."

So she's got some emotional damage. Who doesn't? I get in my moods, and Tracy can be a fucking nightmare. Wasn't gonna stop me from fucking her.

I played with my shirt—didn't know what to say.

"I'm sure Tracy'll be out in a minute."

"There's my girl."

She walked into the room naked. Ellen stood. They embraced—slow, tender.

This is fucking excellent.

Ellen kissed the bandage on Tracy's shoulder.

"Did he hurt my baby," she said.

Tracy put her hands on Ellen's head and pulled her close.

She kissed her—a deep soul kiss like they were alone.

Honestly? I felt jealous—left out.

Tracy noticed. She pulled the coffee table aside and sat next to me on the couch. She leaned in, kissed me, undid my pants and stroked my cock. I couldn't believe this was happening.

She broke our kiss to watch Ellen strip—blouse, bra—*fuck, her tits were perfect. Not too big. Sculpted. Michael-fucking-Angelo tits.*

Ellen dropped to her knees, kissed Tracy's stomach, drifted lower.

When she spread Tracy's legs, Tracy released my cock and leaned into the couch, her breathing matched to Ellen's movement.

Again—uninvolved for the moment—I felt uneasy. Unwanted.

Tracy lifted Ellen's chin. "Do him, baby."

Ellen went down on me.

Fuck man, I was never much of a blow-jobs fan, but Jesus—this bitch could suck a cock. Swallowed me—and I ain't small.

She pulled my pants off without breaking contact, lifted my legs, and gave my ass a tongue bath.

I was worried about the state of my underworks, but she didn't hesitate.

Took me right to the edge three or four times before slipping back to Tracy.

People talk about threesomes like they're easy-peasy—but then they jump in and its awkward, clumsy, not what they imagined.

This wasn't that.

You would'a fucking high-fived me. I was in heaven.

Tracy switched places with Ellen, and knelt between her legs. I leaned in to kiss her childhood friend as Tracy undid Ellen's pants. She looked up at me—there was a moment, a flicker of something—but her eyes said go. Her man enjoying the woman she loved.

I got lost in Ellen.

I felt her lift up as Tracy pulled off her jeans. I could hear her working—slobbering, smacking, devouring Ellen's flesh. She was voracious.

I guess some chicks really let go when they get a chance.

Tracy climbed onto Ellen's lap and shoved me aside.

I'd seen scissoring videos, but this was different—like Tracy was trying to ride her...

"Fuck, Baby—just wait... wait... go slow, Ellie...please."

...like she was imagining Ellen fucking her.

"That's it, baby—bang me like a big girl."

Ellen gripped Tracy's hips and flipped her onto her back. Held her legs up and spread. She stood between them—her majestic cock straining for release.

"WHAT THE FUCK, MAN?"

I jumped off the couch as she entered Tracy. She was inside her—thrusting—while Tracy screamed and moaned.

I grabbed Ellen by the hair and yanked her off. Threw her to the ground.

"What the fuck are you doing?"

Tracy—shocked, scrambled off the couch.

"ARE YOU OUT OF YOUR FUCKING MIND—ELLEN!"

She dropped to her knees beside her.

"Are you okay?"

"I'm okay, baby—just hang on… it's cool."

Ellen got to her feet.

Tracy rose and stepped between us.

"What's wrong with you?"

"She's a fucking dude, man. You're fucking a guy!"

"I am not."

"You're not? So, I guess that was my cock you were sucking on?"

"You're an asshole. And you were kissing her—so what's your fucking problem?"

Ellen stayed quiet.

I felt bad for getting physical.

"I'm sorry. I shouldn't have done that."

"You could've hurt her."

"It's okay, Trace."

Same soft voice, same sweet face.

She slipped her blouse back on, left the rest of her clothes in a pile.

"Why don't we have a drink?" she said.

"I don't drink."

"Okay. Then I'll have one—might help us all calm down."

Tracy looked at me. "That sound good? I've still got half a bottle of red from when my mom was here."

"Yeah sure—fuck it. Why not."

She poured two glasses. We sat back on the couch—Tracy between us.

I'd like to say the silence was awkward, but honestly, I appreciated it. I didn't want to say something fucked. I was uncomfortable, then calm, then uncomfortable again—every time I looked over and saw Ellen sitting with one leg up, her cock—bigger than mine—resting against the cushion.

"I think I'd be doing better if you told me the truth. You weren't eight—you lied. I'm sorry I pulled your hair, Ellen. But all in all, I think I'm doing pretty good."

Tracy kissed me. "You're doing great, baby. I don't know what I was thinking. I should've told you."

Ellen set down her glass. "Better if we just tell him everything."

Tracy stiffened. Ellen squeezed her hand.

"We've been seeing each other for about a month. This was my idea."

"What?"

Tracy jumped in. "I'm sorry, baby. We met at the library. We just clicked. I didn't want to leave you—I still don't. Ellen thought this might help."

"What the fuck is this supposed to help?"

"Oh, come on, guy. At the doctor's office, you were all over me. Don't think I missed how hard it was for you to say you were taken. Looking for a little strange on the side?"

"Fuck you—I haven't done a fucking thing—"

"Other than fucking the delivery girl and letting me suck your cock." She wiped her mouth. "Still got the taste of your mint gum in my throat."

"Fuck you."

Ellen laughed. "We we're heading there. You had to lose it."

I thought about punching her, but you're not supposed to hit girls. I guess if I put a bag over her head, I could punch her in the dick.

"Baby—I..."

"Tracy, don't even say it." I stood and pulled on my clothes. "So what was true?" I looked at Ellen. "Your dad—any of it?"

"Dead. And he did do this." She touched her arm. "He wanted a man, I guess. Got a cunt instead."

"Hmmm, that's a fucking bummer. Anything else—how's that spot on your neck?"

She laughed. "It's not gonna kill me."

I stood there for a minute—weighing my options.

"You got anything, Tracy? Is this what you want?"

"I want both of you. She gives me something you don't. Maybe she's got something for you too."

I guess I was wrong. I'd been telling you to high-five me—and now I'm the one wondering what the fuck happened.

I picked up my car keys.

"Don't leave, baby," Tracy said. "I love you."

I looked at Ellen—she *was* pretty.

She reminded me of a question I used to ask at the bar. One of those, fuck-marry-kill, deals.

I'd find a straight guy—you can never really tell, but you know the type, and I'd ask: Okay, there's no way out of this. You gotta fuck one of 'em. Is it Cindy Crawford with an 8" inch cock, or Chuck Norris with a pussy?

You should've seen those assholes squirm. They didn't know which way to go.

Hell, I used to wonder what way I'd go…

…until I found out.

I picked up Ellen's glass of wine, took a sip, and got myself undressed.

The Executioners

They assembled on the fence behind O'Malley's. The meeting was prearranged. Roll call was taken.

"Gritz?"

"Here."

"Ziggy?"

"Here."

"Mr. Boots?"

"Here."

"Jasper?... Jasper?... Has anyone seen Jasper?"

"I saw him Tuesday," said Boots. "He was lying on the street near the school. One of those little fuckers on 12th had placed a *Free Cat* sign on the parkway above his head."

This announcement was met with angry wails of feline displeasure. Cinnamon Joe was irate.

"I say we do those little pricks right after we settle tonight's business. No more pussy-footing around—let's take it to 'em."

"All agreed?" said the leader, a one-eyed tom that ran by the name of Bernard.

"Agreed!"

The business that Cinnamon Joe was referring to was what to do with the canine on Mulberry. A week before, she'd escaped her leash and caught a strolling Gritz by the throat.

"This thing itches," said Gritz.

The plastic cone around his neck was cumbersome and stiff.

"Twenty-five stitches I got from that bitch. Do you know how hard it is to groom yourself with this fucking cone on?" He attempted to nibble his bits in demonstration. "It's payback time for that fucking mutt."

"You got that right," said Ziggy. "What do you think... poison?"

The others nodded in approval.

"And how are you gonna get him to eat it—or get it to him, for that matter?" Bernard strolled the fence. "What are you gonna do, walk it over on your hind legs and drop it in his bowl? No. We need something simpler, less obvious."

"I've got an idea," said Gritz, "a real clean little plan and nobody will be the wiser. Listen up."

The plan was introduced, discussed, and accepted by all.

"And that's that," said Bernard.

He licked the back of his paw.

"We'll meet on the corner of Elm and Pecan at 6 p.m. Don't be late."

The meeting was adjourned, and light refreshments were served courtesy of the dumpster behind the fish house.

At 6 p.m. they met on the aforementioned corner and paraded their way to Mulberry Street.

Ziggy jumped the fence and quietly chewed at the intended victim's rope, weakening the hemp.

They wanted it to break—but only after some resistance. Accidents can happen, and this mangy mutt had been known to be dangerous.

Mr. Boots jumped on the gate and lifted the latch with his paw.

All was ready.

"Meow," wailed Mr. Boots from on top the gate. "Meow!" he cried.

The murderous canine crept from her doghouse and spotted the wailing cat. She leapt.

"Woof, woof, woof!"

She charged forward, hitting the end of her rope—violently yanked off her feet and slammed to the ground.

"WOOF, WOOF, WOOF!"

Eyes wild, she strained against the hemp—yanking and biting and straining—and…snap! It broke!

She was free.

The crazed dog crashed into the unlocked gate and burst onto the sidewalk.

Mr. Boots dashed into the bushes.

Gritz, stationed on the corner, picked up the call.

"Meow," he wailed. "Meow!"

The scent of the injured Gritz inflamed her fury. Mad she ran at the bright orange tabby.

He backed into the street.

The beast rolled on.

Gritz moved onto the center of the roadway.

The beast neared.

"Meow," Gritz wailed as the tire of a passing car lightly swiped his cone.

The beast advanced.

Consumed with the fur ball she should have previously dispatched, her great jaws gaped—strings of puppy chow saliva hanging like vicious stalactites.

The target was near.

Gritz held his ground.

A large city bus moved heavy. Unaware.

The beast ran wild into the roadway.

"WOOF! WOOF! WOOF!"

Gritz was moments away from destruction and then— EEEEEEK—a sharp squeal of brakes, a loud THUMP... and the hound was no more.

Melded to the asphalt, pinned under the wheels of city bus 134.

The executioners gathered on the sidewalk. The deed was done. The sentence rendered.

"And now for those brats on 12th."

Cinnamon Joe licked his whiskers. The scent of roadkill puppy in the air.

"Children love playing in the street. It shouldn't be hard."

ALSO, BY JACK GRISHAM

AN AMERICAN DEMON
UNTAMED
CODE BLUE—A LOVE STORY
I WISH THERE WERE MONSTERS
A PRINCIPLE OF RECOVERY
THE PULSE OF THE WORLD
TRANSMISSION
THE COFFEE MAKER

AVAILABLE WORLDWIDE